Written by
William Kirtland

Illustrated by
Consuelo Udave

Published by
Idaho Book and School Supply
5286 Chinden Blvd.
Boise, Idaho 83714

Printed by
SHERIDAN BOOKS
613 E. Industrial Drive
Chelsea, Michigan 48118-0370

Special Thanks

Bette Joy, Lamont Lyons,
Nancy Roberts, Willie Stittsworth
and Gladys Talbott

To

Margaret and Henry

CHAPTER 1
Toot-Toot

It was a beautiful spring day. A freshness filled the air. The sun shone brilliantly on the gravel road with pieces of shadows stretched here and there. As we rounded the bend in the road in our burial caravan, a certain blackness overcame the sunlight and there to our left we saw many gray stones all clumped together. I will never forget the many times we had played leapfrog over those markers.

D. J. Appleton had the biggest stone and it was hardest to clear. Several times my pants were torn by the edge of his marker. Then the boys would say, "Hey, old man Appleton tore your pants," or "Dusty will get you tonight for stepping on his grave." And then that night I would dream about old D. J. Appleton coming up the stairs after me. Some nights he would have a long beard and terrible-looking straggly hair and on other nights he would be just a white skeleton with a long sheet draped over his bones.

As we pulled into the cemetery, I brought our car to a sudden stop and old Dusty Appleton faded out of my mind. There stood Father Riley very solemn looking, all fancy in his garb. He had a gold pail that contained holy water, and the little altar boy next to him carried a dish with a small spoon on it. I knew this held the ashes and that Father Riley would soon be saying, "Remember, old man, you are dust and to dust thou shalt return." This saying I knew by heart, as I had carried that little dish many times. I had helped many priests. We had buried a lot of people, including old D. J. Appleton.

My mother got out of the car and her pretty blue shoes squeezed into the spring mud. She was completely unaware of the soft damp ground. Ordinarily, she always wanted to be sure not to park near the mud puddles and usually made quite a fuss about it if one did, but not this time.

I grasped her arm and we walked over by Father Riley and the altar boy who stood near his side.

"Good morning, Father," my mother said. My mother was always thoughtful and polite, especially to nuns and priests, and today was no different.

We proceeded toward a mound of fresh clay. There was a cheap piece of imitation grass stretched over the pile, which was uneven. It looked as though it had been just tossed there. As we got closer to the mound, we could see down into the hole. It appeared dark and damp. Every so often clumps of moist clay were dropping here and there to the bottom.

As we looked to our left, we could see six men approaching us from a small cement house. This cement house is where my father's body had been all winter. When he died, he could not be buried until spring because the ground was frozen down, some said, nearly five feet. Sven Carlson used to dig those graves and I overheard him several times in the gas station saying it was a very tough job digging in December, January, and February.

Sven said that there were times when he had to burn over twenty tires just to soften the ground so he could dig one grave. He received $12.50 for each grave and would blow the whole sum in the gas station playing gin rummy with the boys. I beat him many times and took that grave-digging money away from him. I remember one time taking him for ninety-three cents in one game. I will never forget his remark, "Well, there goes about two feet from old Adelle Peterson's grave." That night I took the money and threw it in the river on my way home. I sure did not want old widow Peterson coming up the stairway after me like D. J. Appleton.

The six men were getting closer now and there was my father's casket, all blue and trimmed in gold. My mother was sniffling and the tears started running down my cheeks. I just could not stop them.

My father was a railroad man, a section foreman. He was very hard working. To many people, he came across as being especially mean and cranky. He always wore a pair of

2

blue bib overalls that were baggy at the rear. The bib had special pockets that were filled with pencils, pens, and old sheets of train orders.

He swore a lot, too much to suit my mother; and at times it was downright embarrassing, especially when our fancy relatives, the priest, or company came to the house. When he would get to telling a railroad tale, all of us would hold our breath for fear of the language he might use. For some strange reason those people who we were so worried about always encouraged him to tell his stories. I am not sure whether they enjoyed looking at our faces or hearing the stories my dad told.

He was a good man in many ways. He was always very concerned about the amount of food we had on our table. He really enjoyed good things to eat; and if my mother had not put up over one hundred quarts of blueberries for the winter, he would storm and holler around the house predicting that it was going to be one long winter this year, and we had better be prepared for it.

He nearly always called me Billy. "Billy," he would say, "you are not going to be a railroad man like me. You are going places, Billy; why you will probably be our next governor." My dad would then cup his hands and chant, "Mr. Speaker, Mr. Speaker, the governor of the great State of Minnesota, the Honorable Billy F. Kirtland!" My sister, Lois, would sit by the kitchen stove and snicker about my father's prediction.

The six men slid the pretty blue casket into a cement vault, which I insisted my mother buy, as I did not want the water and mud leaking into his coffin. I whispered to my mother, "Does he have his watches?" and she merely nodded. I knew this would be important to him.

He always carried two watches and sometimes three just for safety purposes, depending on the time of the year. We used to have daylight-savings time during the summer, and God knows my dad hated that daylight-savings time. He used to say, "Those rich dudes in the cities who want to play golf should get up an hour earlier; we shouldn't have to be punished for their fancy needs." The two watches were carried because one was set for daylight-savings time and one for standard or railroad time. He used to get lots of calls from people downtown inquiring about when the train was arriving. Those calls made him plenty sore. The callers found it hard to understand if the passenger left St. Paul at 8:30 p.m. standard time, and assuming that it would not lose or gain any time, the train should arrive in Littlefork at 7:30 a.m. standard time. The railroad never switched to daylight-savings time so when the confused public wanted the daylight version and inquired whether it was really late or not, he would say, "Just be at the depot at 6:00 tomorrow morning either time and you'll make it." After he set the receiver down, he would say, "Let those stupid dumbbells stand by the depot and wait till hell freezes over, for all I care." After a number of calls, everyone and everything became so confused that my dad started carrying two watches, one set for daylight-savings time and the other set for standard time. The extra watch seemed to help him and the people calling.

Yes, it used to be some fun to hear him on the phone explaining the time the train would be in. When a few of us didn't have anything else to do for entertainment, we would call my dad from the gas station downtown and fake like we were the banker or some citizen expecting to take a trip, and ask him when the train was coming in. He would start out real civil-like but once we couldn't understand what he was talking about, wow! How he would cuss and raise a storm!

The six men were having some time with the huge concrete box, but finally slid the whole works over to the opening while the priest was making the sign of the cross. We all prayed several "Our Fathers" and "Hail Marys." Then the priest sprinkled holy water on the concrete box. All of this had a special meaning to each of us.

I sure was relieved that he had his watches, as he looked at them so frequently; the correct time is an important part of a railroad man's life. We often sat in the house on cold winter evenings and heard the switch engine down by the depot moving boxcars back and forth. In fact, we not only could hear the train, but we could feel it vibrate right in the section house. The whole house would creak and shake. Even the water in the water pail would make little ripples and the glasses in our cupboard would tremble when the train was switching. And as the freight train came into town, my father would pull out his watch, glance at it and then sit back, roll a cigarette, and read the paper. After about thirty-five to forty minutes all would be quiet and my father would pull out his watch again. Then two short toots would shrill their way up toward our house. My dad would take another glance at his watch and say, "Well, their work is done here; it's all over. That's the `high ball' and they are moving on."

Just then Father Riley said, "Remember, old man, you are dust and to dust thou shalt return." My mother began to turn away from the ceremony. I looked down into the grave and as I pulled my head up to turn toward my mother, I could hear way off in the distance the switch engine by the depot; and it said, "Toot! Toot!"

CHAPTER 2
The Accident

Our journey from the cemetery back home was very gloomy and sad. Down through Main Street we went. This time it wasn't the pleasant Main Street that I had grown to love. Our funeral caravan looked larger now with well over fifty cars. The custom was to return to the house, sit around, and attempt to make it through the day. Everyone said that the first day would be the toughest and from there on things would get better and easier.

As we drove up to the yard, the reminiscing began. My mother suggested that Hank would be pretty proud of the turnout. Even Frank Guerin was there and heaven knows Dad and Frank Guerin had their disagreements. As we stepped out of the car, I could just make out the caboose at least three miles up the track. Yes, truly their work was done and they were on their way.

Once we arrived at the house, things were somewhat easier. Mrs. Gottsacker was pouring coffee and there was a brightness with all the people gathered around, some sniffling, some laughing and some not really knowing what to do or say.

Each person came to us in private. "Your dad was one heck of a guy." "We'll miss him." "Well, Hank had a big day, all the flowers and that turnout. I've never seen anything like it." To the last person there was a special remembrance.

As the distant friends left and said good-by, just the relatives were left; and as evening approached, there remained only the four of us--my two sisters, Lois and Pat, and my mother and me.

We all cried a little as we talked about the good times, the tough times, the happy times. For each of us it was a reflection on our past.

My mother said, "I will never forget the time when the five of us lived in our little two-room railroad shack just

7

outside of International Falls." She sat red-eyed in the living room rocker.

"Your dad was truly the man of the house. He was a section laborer on the Northern Pacific Railway. He had just been transferred to the Falls for his first steady job with the company. In those times a steady job was not too easy to be found, so he considered himself most fortunate. The $55 a month was big money, especially when one considered the Depression that had just come to an end. Your dad was awarded the job on the basis of his loyal part-time service. Of course, the fact that Grandpa Kirtland was a hard-working section foreman certainly helped him get hired in the first place."

We all looked at the various sympathy cards and Lois and Pat began writing thank-you notes.

My mother kept rocking and talking. She continued to bring up the early days. It was good therapy for her. She was wound up.

"When your dad came into the house that Friday evening, he was completely exhausted after having put in nearly sixty-six ties. `This work is for a plow horse,' he commented as he sat at our meager supper table. `But at least I've got a job, Margaret.'

"With almost every other sentence he'd say, `Margaret, you've got to be sure to remember to watch those kids so that they don't get out on the tracks,' and continued to eat his wieners, sauerkraut and boiled potato supper.

"That night, like every night, you kids were playing on the floor in the living room," my mother added. "Lois, I'm ashamed to say it but you always wore little brown stockings with holes in the knees. Your hair was chopped off short like a boy's. Pattie, you were only a month-old baby at the time. I must say your arrival was a little unexpected." We all laughed at that comment. "Billy, you were sixteen months old, just able to walk and plenty full of mischief." My mom talked on with tears in her eyes.

"Finally I lured you kids to bed, put some hot water in the dish pan, and began to wash the supper dishes. I was always exhausted from my long day's work. I never really did that much but always seemed to be tired. I was very pleased to crawl in bed beside your dad. He was always snoring like he lived in the Ozarks.

"That next morning your dad and I were up at the crack of dawn as always. I fixed him pancakes and eggs. He always ate his breakfast in his shorts or long underwear. His hairy legs made quite a spectacle. Of course, you all know that. You know that there were some mornings in the winter when we all ate wearing our coats and mittens.

"'Margaret, someday we will be out of this terrible life. When I get to be a section foreman, we will then have a section house just like Ma and Pa. Probably we can have a cow, some chickens and even a garden.' He constantly promised us a better life.

"As he left the bunkhouse he kissed me good-by for the day. He was immediately on the job, as we were surrounded with railroad tracks. He walked slowly down toward the motorcar house where the speeders, push cars, and railroad tools were housed. I couldn't help but be proud of my little man and the way his bib overalls tossed from side to side as he moved out of sight," my mother said.

"As I began my morning routine, I discovered that we were out of drinking water. I knew that you kids were all sleeping, so I thought now would be as good a time as any to take the walk across the tracks to the community pump. As I left the bunkhouse, I took a little piece of wire and inserted it through the screen door, causing the hook to drop through the loop and as a result locked the door behind me. I just never should have left you kids like that, but I did," my mother said.

"As I crossed those five sets of tracks, I looked back to see that everything was all right. With each step the smell of oil and creosote touched my nostrils. When I reached the pump, I was happy that I had remembered to save enough water so I wouldn't have to walk way down by the roundhouse for priming water.

"While I pumped water into the pail, I looked up the tracks and approaching the yards' office was a railroad observation car pulling two push car loads of ties. It was a heavy load and the cars screeched and groaned as they came closer.

"I continued to pump the water; and as I did, an object on my left caught my eye. I moved my head in the direction of our bunkhouse, and there in the center of the third track stood Billy. I was weak and breathless, stopped pumping, and set out on a dead run toward Bill. He was not twenty feet from me, dressed only in his little under shorts.

"I could plainly see that Billy was closer to me than he was to the observation car that was fast approaching. I believed I had a good chance. In fact, he was more than two tracks away from the oncoming car. As I got closer to Bill and he saw me coming, he turned and began to run back toward our house. That's where I guess I made another big mistake, chasing him.

"I don't know what went on in his little head. I wondered why he was running away from me. Perhaps he thought we were playing games as we did during the lonely days and nights. In any case, he darted back in the direction of the tracks where the observation car was coming.

"As I ran toward Billy, he also picked up speed. Ray Gibson, who was driving the observation car, began to sound his horn and apply his brakes. There was no stopping the car as it began to slide down the tracks, with the iron wheels on the steel tracks making a terrible loud squeal.

"Billy was no match for the car, but it seemed he thought so as he stood in the center of the tracks holding up his little fists and laughing.

"When the observation car struck him, it knocked him to my side of the tracks; and I just stood there and watched frantically. I fell to my knees as I saw him being thrown into the cinders. As he left the tracks, his arm went under the first

wheel, then another and another until six wheels had crossed his arm causing three fingers to fall into the cinders inside the tracks. His arm was all mangled and his head was bleeding terribly. When I finally reached him, he was on my side of the tracks just motionless.

"I picked him up. First, I sat down and rocked my baby boy, hoping he would be okay. Then I began to run toward the motorcar house where your dad was working. Henry had seen the accident and was approaching me with that crazy look he used to get in his eyes when he was really mad. Ray Gibson had finally brought his load to a stop; he came out of the car staggering and hollering, `Get a doctor! Get a doctor! Good God, I didn't mean to hit that kid. Where did he come from?'

"Dad tore Bill from my arms, swearing and carrying on just like a mad bull. He immediately ran for town with Billy in his arms. I ran after him falling over the tracks. We were all in a state of wildness. Bill's arm was draped over Dad's shoulder, and blood was spurting down Dad's back. A man driving by the highway crossing also saw the accident and quickly motioned to Henry to come and get into his Model A Ford. Your dad, Billy and I, and the driver all went as fast as we could in his car toward town and the doctor's office.

"By the time we reached the doctor's office, we could see that Bill had turned pale white. We were sure that he was dead, but we had hope that the good Lord would help us, that by some stroke of luck a miracle might occur.

"Dad rushed into the doctor's office, and the nurse guided him into a back room. There were no people in the office, mostly because folks in town considered this new, young doctor too different and too modern to suit them. In fact, he had already been labeled a 'horse doctor'; your dad was one person who called him that several times. But it was different now, as the most popular doctor was way across town and Dad knew there was no time to shop around.

"I handed the doctor Billy's fingers that I had picked up and had clenched in my hands, in hopes that in some way they might be fastened back to his little hand. The doctor told me it was too late for them. I was just sick to my stomach.

"Dr. Moore washed Billy's arm while both Dad and I stood by aiding in any way that we could. Finally Billy came to and he began to cry with the sickest, mournful moan. It was a soft sob that nearly broke our hearts. After that I could never stand to hear or see him cry.

"`Mr., Mrs. Kirtland, I think we are going to have to take that arm off; I'm afraid of infection,' the doctor said. I dropped to my knees and fainted. I was carried to a lounge in the outer office.

"Dad and the doctor discussed Billy's chances and finally agreed to gamble on a new idea that Dr. Moore had just learned in medical school. Dr. Moore sewed the arm up the best he could; in all it took 133 stitches. He then bandaged Billy's arm to his stomach. His arm stayed that way until the skin from his stomach had attached to the raw flesh of his arm. They called it a new type of skin graft. After six hours of surgery, Billy and I were taken by ambulance to the Falls hospital. I never left his side.

"That night Billy passed in and out of consciousness, and in the morning his condition was pronounced very low. A priest was called and last rites were administered. Your father and I were both clenched together in tears during the last rites. We almost gave up hope.

"I lit a candle and stayed on my knees into the morning hours. I don't know how many Hail Marys I said. At about 9:00 that morning, Billy opened his eyes and began to talk. He whispered that he wanted some `wato.' Throughout that day he seemed to look better. As the hours passed, he continued to make steady improvement until by the third day he was up and running around with his bad arm bandaged to his stomach and his right arm free and willing to play.

"While in the hospital, Dad and I gave each other much needed support. `At least he has something, Margaret. Why, give him some time, that hand will straighten out even if it is missing three fingers,' Dad whispered.

"Your dad kept saying, `Don't blame yourself, Margaret. It wasn't your fault!' But I always felt guilty over that accident. I still can't get over how careless I was.

"Day by day Billy slowly recovered. He was in the hospital over three months. When he came home, we all had to adjust to his bad hand. I cried about it plenty but tried never to let you know about that, Bill. Dr. Moore worked closely with us during the first year.

"While in Dr. Moore's office, we were lectured about forcing Bill to use those two fingers whenever possible. Dr. Moore used to throw pennies on the floor; Billy picked them up with his two fingers. I remember Dr. Moore saying, `Folks, this child should be able to do nearly everything that any normal child can do, if you will encourage him.' I know your dad never babied you about your hand, Bill. We had lots of quarrels about what you could or couldn't do, but Dad always insisted you could do it.

"Dad and I were sure two sick parents. The railroad company paid all the bills. I remember Dad saying, `Not only did they cover the bills, but they deposited $1,000 in the bank for Billy when he goes to college. And he will go to college. One thing I can promise you, he will never work on the railroad!'"

By now my mother's eyes were a very deep red, redder than when she usually tried to tell the story. Before, she would always try to tell it but could never finish it. That night she finished the story to the very end.

"The accident almost took the starch out of your dad and me," my mother said. "He never mentioned it but I believe that's how we came to move from International Falls back to Bemidji. Your dad took the tower job; it was a night job with less pay, but it meant a home further away from the tracks for all of us and a front yard for you kids to play in.

"You kids meant a lot to Dad. He wanted the best for you. I know he used to go crazy with those lickings, but he loved you so much it was only his way to teach you. He used to cry lots of times when he would take you to the woodshed, Bill; you'll never know."

CHAPTER 3
Pussy Willow Switch

We bought a three-room house in Bemidji. Our house had a blue-shingled roof. We lived in a section of Bemidji called Mill Park.

Mill Park sat on a hill about fifty feet above two lakes. We were enclosed like a peninsula. Not only were we surrounded by water, but there were four sets of railroad tracks that completely isolated us from the rest of the town. I always believed that we were located in the prettiest and best part of the town; however, I remember hearing incidental comments that we lived in the low-class part of the town. None of us folks who lived there believed that or understood what was meant by low-class.

Everyone in our family was very proud of our $900 home. It was the only house in the area with blue shingles. The rest of the houses in Mill Park had tarpapered roofs, so we thought we were something special. We used to drive around in the summer evenings just looking at the roofs of the houses; and my dad often said, "You know what? We have the only blue-shingled roof in Bemidji," my dad didn't mention that the paint he used to make that roof blue came from the Northern Pacific Railway. We all knew it but no one dared breathe a word about our advantage.

My mother went out to the kitchen to fix some coffee while Pat and Lois continued on with the thank-you cards. I couldn't help but get the reminiscing going again when I said, "Mom, do you remember the lickin' I got from Dad over that boat on Lake Irving? How old was I? About eight or nine?"

It was a Saturday morning, and I had my slingshot in my overall's hind pocket. In my front pockets were about twenty-five well-chosen rocks for ammunition.

I strolled down the sidewalk making sure not to step on any cracks to avoid breaking my mother's back (as the saying went) and not stepping on any lines so I wouldn't break my mother's clothesline. Occasionally I drew my slingshot, pulled back the rubbers until I couldn't pull any harder, and let go, clinking the mailbox of old man Harding. Old man Harding hated kids and made it a point to keep any ball that bounced into his yard. Anytime we got a good game going, you could bet that someone would hit or kick the ball into old man Harding's yard and then out he would come, his little belt tight around his potbelly and his suspenders draped over his shoulders for safety purposes, pick up the ball and scoot back to his house. His wife, old lady Harding, would sit on the front porch and swing back and forth on a kind of wooden-like couch supported by four chains that were fastened to the roof of the porch. The belief was that each evening the Hardings would go down in their basement and count all the balls they had taken from the kids. Then along about Christmas time, Christmas Eve to be exact, they would throw all of the balls into the furnace and they would dance for joy, celebrating the festive season. Boy, how I hated those Hardings and worst of all we lived right next door to them.

In the next house on the other side of us lived the Bergstroms. They, too, were older people. They had a son named Milo. Milo was about as old as my father, I guess. He was really weird and every kid in Mill Park was scared to death of him. Every time we saw him, we would yell, "Milo, Milo, where's your silo?" and then we would run like the dickens, with him right behind us.

One time when I came home at night, I looked through the kitchen window and there was Milo talking to my dad and mother. I was petrified, thinking that he was telling them about how I teased him, so I sneaked into my bedroom by the back way, slipped under the covers and laid there listening to their conversation.

Milo was stammering away in the kitchen, talking about how his mother and dad were so mean to him. I never knew that before so it came as a complete surprise to me. All of a sudden I heard my dad say, "Something's wrong with

Milo, Margaret." I sat up quickly in bed afraid that Milo was coming into my bedroom to choke me or something. Then I heard the craziest commotion. I jumped to my feet and looked out into the kitchen; and there on the floor was Milo, just frothing at the mouth with my father on top of him. His feet were kicking and his arms were thrashing about. He was kicking so hard that he kicked a big, black mark on our kitchen cabinets in his wildness. My father was jamming a spoon into his mouth. My mother was shouting and carrying on so, that I began to cry and holler, as I was sure Milo was trying to kill my dad. Then all of a sudden Milo became less and less violent until he was completely relaxed. Then my father said, while glaring at me, "Get that kid out of here so he doesn't see this." Later I learned that Milo had had an epileptic seizure. My dad told me, "If you ever tell anyone about this, I'll take you to the woodshed and give you a sound licking." I never did breathe a word of it. It wasn't any fun after that to call, "Milo, Milo, where's your silo?"

As I proceeded down the sidewalk, I finally came to my very special friend's house. Wally Nelson was the kind of guy one really liked. He was tough and big and he was my protector. I could say anything to anyone and could always count on Wally coming to my rescue. He was good at everything and very athletic. Try as I might, I could rarely beat him at running, basketball, knife, whatever it was; he was that good. There was one exception, however, that being marbles. He was good at marbles all right, but I was better. I still lost to him though, because if he came home with fewer marbles than he left the house with, his mother, Faye, would make him practice by the hours in the dining room. Consequently, I used to let him beat me on purpose. If he had to practice by the hours, then I couldn't come into his house or we wouldn't be able to go outside together. As a result, I was the one that was punished if he won or lost.

As I rapped on Wally's screen door, I could see that the Nelson's porch was slowly rotting away; and I wondered how long they would be able to live in that house in the condition it was in. Faye came to the door--she always did--and she opened it, so I walked in, which I always did even without being invited. I knew that if I said, "Is Wally home?" she would say, "He's sleeping," or "Wait outside and I'll tell him you're here." When that happened, I would have to sit on that porch for what seemed like endless hours just kicking the dirt. I soon discovered that being polite was not the best way; so, as usual, I just walked right in, past Faye.

When I got inside the house, I sat down on the brown leather davenport that had big face carvings on each arm. This is where I always sat when I was in the house. I could hear Wally and his dad in the kitchen eating breakfast; the smell of burned toast was in the air. The Nelsons had a toaster that they had to change by hand, and sometimes Faye would forget her job. Apparently this was one of her mornings. Frank was a real swell guy. He was so tall it was hard to believe a man could be that big, and he had a smile like you never saw before. His blue eyes seemed to sparkle; he was just plain likable, even though he almost always had a two-day growth on his face. This particular morning they were having their usual oatmeal, toast, and coffee. Wally drank coffee like nobody's business. I often wondered how he could stand that black, greasy coffee, burned toast, and oatmeal covered with thick canned milk. Just the sight of that Holstein cow pictured on the milk can would almost cause me to throw up right on the spot.

As they sat there eating, I looked around the room. They had a coal heater in the living room with a wooden chair on each side of it. Across the room, right in front of me, was a brown china closet with all kinds of pictures, cups and saucers, and newspaper clippings. In the center of the china closet was a picture of a navy man who was fat and jovial-looking. He was Wally's brother. He was the brother that Wally always bragged about. Wally said that when his big brother drank a lot of beer, he could write his name "George" by peeing in the snow. I often thought that was about the greatest achievement I knew, as I could never get beyond the first letter, "B", in my name.

To the left of the brown china closet was a basket that was made of bamboo and in it were about five very unhealthy geraniums. There were always about five or six dried-up yellow leaves on the floor. Covering the floor was a linoleum rug with a flower pattern in it. Where the doors entered the kitchen, bedroom or upstairs, the roses were pretty well worn down to just black tar paper. The walls, too, were covered with flowers, little tiny ones of gold and tan. Here and there the wallpaper was either cracked or frayed.

I sat many times looking at that room just waiting for Wally. Finally he came. He had his slingshot and he, too, had his pockets full of rocks, so I knew that we were on our way for a real fun day. We really never knew which way we were going, but what was the difference? We had so many places to explore. No matter which way we turned, we would find plenty to shoot at and much to talk about.

We decided to go to Little Woods, which was across the Great Northern tracks and down by Lake Irving. There were lots of blackbirds there that we could kill and maybe we could play "Indian", too. We had a cave over there that consisted of a 10-foot hole in the sandbank. There we sometimes sat for hours whittling out slingshot crotches or making willow whistles.

As we proceeded down the tracks, we saw a cedar waxwing on the telephone wire. Wally was first to shoot, and pufft! he hit her dead center. She went down fluttering, losing her feathers as she fell. He ran over to look at it. She was soft and warm with a little blood running out of her eye and beak. I kicked a hole in the ground for burial purposes while Wally took out his knife and etched a notch in his slingshot. He must have had 60 notches on the crotch of his slingshot.

As we stood there burying the bird, not 30 feet from us was a boat that was beached by the shore of the lake. We took a couple of potshots at it trying to hit the water close by so as to make the water splash into the boat. We walked down by the boat and fooled around for a few minutes. Wally jumped in and I pushed us out by kneeling down on the front seat. Soon we were drifting about 10 feet from the shore. We only had one oar that we used to pole our way around while looking down at the bottom of the lake.

Occasionally we could see minnows darting here and there in the weeds. As we poled around, we got farther and farther away from shore. Just then the freight train came by and we watched the cars as they zoomed along. I temporarily forgot that my dad's friends all worked on the railroad; and before I remembered, I saw Shorty Oftedahl, the brakeman, standing outside the caboose. He waved to us. As he waved, I tried to duck so he couldn't see me.

Just as I ducked down, Wally put the oar down in the soft sand. My sudden movement caused the boat to rock, and his hand let go of the oar. We were now drifting helplessly on Lake Irving. We both looked at each other somewhat amazed and startled. I immediately started to whine, for that was my only defense. Almost as soon as I began sniffling, Wally broke down, too; and then I really began to see the seriousness of the matter, as I had never heard him whimper.

By this time, we were well away from shore. I looked down at the bottom of the lake and discovered we were in deep water. This made me feel more uneasy as I quickly sat down in the boat. As I did so, the boat again rocked back and forth and Wally almost lurched forward into the lake.

As we sat there helpless, we discovered that there was a tiny film of water on the bottom of the boat. We noticed the water coming in because our shoes began to feel damp and cold. I looked around the boat and discovered that in the back of the boat was a whittled-out plug, with a piece of old underwear squeezed into an apparent rotted-out knothole. Upon a closer look I discovered that water was trickling in around the plug. I kicked at the plug, trying to pound it in further, but as I hit the plug the water began to flow into the boat at a much faster rate. By now the water was well over the soles of our shoes and we were crying the likes of which we had never cried before. We hollered and shouted up toward Mill Park but it seemed no one heard us.

By this time we had been adrift for about an hour and were forced to stand on the boat seats. We waved our hands back and forth. Finally I could barely make out a human figure by the shore of the lake.

The person had managed to find another boat, and we saw him rowing frantically out toward us. I was so relieved to see him coming, as I knew all would soon be well. As he came closer and closer I began to say to Wally, "No, it can't be!" But is was; it was my dad! He had the meanest look on his face; his eyes were set and I knew that he would soon tear me apart.

Now I had a new fear. I wished I had fallen over and drowned rather than to have to face my dad, for he had forbidden me to ever go by the lakes, the tracks, Little Woods, and every other place that tempted me.

My dad finally got up close and hollered to us, "Sit down in that boat, you two." He was swearing and grumbling so, that the air was blue. I was so scared that I began to tremble. He eased his boat next to ours. With his one hand holding onto our boat, he reached for us one at a time to put us in his boat.

As he put me in his boat, he squeezed my arm so hard that I felt numbness right down to my feet. He didn't say a word to either of us as he rowed us back to shore. With every paddle, he stared directly at me. By now every neighbor in Mill Park was standing on the hill to witness the scene.

When we hit shore, I jumped out of the boat; and as my foot hit the sand, my father let the first swat fly. He hit my backside so hard that I fell forward onto the wet beach. My rear was hurting like a hundred bees had stung me all at once. In one fast turnabout, I was up and running for our house with my dad right on my heels, knocking me down as I'd get up to run. He told Wally to go to his own house and to tell his parents what had happened.

The hits didn't seem to hurt as much as having all of this happen right in front of everyone on the hill. In spite of the fact that I didn't want them to see or hear the show, I began to scream and holler, "No Dad, no Dad," crying and bleating to his hitting rhythm.

By this time my mother jumped in front of my dad. She was holding my father back by his shoulders, trying to pull him off of me. How glad I was to see her!

I managed to run for our house and hide under my bed, but within seconds he came at me again. This time he had a green pussy willow switch and he said, "Get to the woodshed!"

My mother was right behind him and she was sobbing, "No, Henry, that's enough," but I knew there was no stopping him now.

I didn't feel as sorry for myself as I did for my mother. I knew that she was in worse pain than me. She had the saddest look on her face and little parts of her chin were quivering. She, too, was crying. I knew that her eyes said I had received enough. I wanted her to quit crying so badly, but there was nothing I could do. Finally I walked bravely and slowly to the woodshed so she wouldn't think I had been treated so harshly. I hoped this might help her relieve her feelings.

I went to the woodshed like a man with my dad behind me switching me on my rear. I didn't make one reaction to the hits, still in hopes my mother would be under the impression that it didn't hurt. As I rounded the corner to the woodshed, I began to dance and yell, for I couldn't take those piercing, stinging, switches any longer.

I don't know how long we were in there, but it seemed like hours and hours. Finally the only way I could get him to stop was to put my hand--my crippled hand--out in front of his switch hoping he would quit. He swung very hard; and as he did so, the tiny little ends of the pussy willow switch laid into the soft pink grafted skin of my left hand. This caused my bad hand to bleed terribly. My father began to back off. I put on a little extra act just for safety purposes and screamed, "My hand, my hand!" My dad immediately fell to his knees and put his hand over his mouth. As he did this he breathed through his hand making loud sucking sounds.

As I took one look at him on his knees in the woodshed, I could see the tears flowing down his cheeks, and, now I felt worse than ever. I ran to the house and climbed into my bed sobbing. Little did I know that my father remained out there in the woodshed. My mother waited well past midnight for him until he finally came in worn out with grief.

I prayed so hard that night. "Please, God, help me to be a good boy. Please, God, help me to be a good boy. Please, God, help my dad so he doesn't get so mad at me, and don't let my mom cry like that again."

Finally, I dropped off to sleep.

CHAPTER 4
Gone Fishing

The licking I received in that woodshed was awfully hard to forget. It seemed like weeks passed before I could really get it out of my mind. I always saw to it that the wood box was filled and even spent some time weeding the garden on my own. Slowly other forces took over, and it wasn't too long before digging angleworms, watching the acorns grow, and killing swallows began to occupy my mind more than the licking. The acorns represented spending money when brought to the zoo, and the angleworms were picked for my bait business.

All of my collection of angleworms motivated me to try my luck at the sunfish hole downtown by the bridges. I knew that the bluegills could not resist those big, juicy worms. After picking at least another five dozen, I began to get my tackle ready. I hadn't looked at my tackle box since the summer before and it showed it. Inside the rectangular, black converted dinner pail were three rusty hooks, two sinkers with the ears pinched tight, and a big bass plug that I had found washed up on the shore of Lake Irving. I never had the opportunity to use the bass plug, as I didn't have a casting or trolling rod; and I never had the chance to go fishing in a boat. There was some red and white paint left on my Daredevil, but one of the treble hooks was missing. It didn't matter about the condition of the Daredevil, though, as I was truly proud of that lure and always felt it was very impressive-looking in my box.

My bamboo pole was split at the end, but I knew it would do if I were to put some of my dad's friction tape on the end of it. Before I knew it, I was making plans to go fishing.

I sneaked into the house and rummaged around for a cork. I knew my mother had several extras that she used for my father's thermos bottles. I took the butcher knife and split the cork halfway and then took a wooden match that was used to attach my line to the cork. My dad taught me how to make this type of bobber, and I was appreciative of his instruction.

I was all set. That night I went to bed early. All I could think of was the fun I would have catching fish the next day. Lying in that little cot dreaming about my catch was most enjoyable. Throughout the night I would wake up, see that it was still very dark, go back to sleep, wake up, doze off again, until finally it became light.

It didn't take a minute to dress as all I wore was my bib overalls. In the summer, shoes and shirt were not a part of my wardrobe. These would come later when school started, as wearing those items in the fall was soon enough for me.

I left the house quietly with my pole, tackle box, and can of worms. I walked down the sidewalk, past Bergstroms toward the lumberyard. When I reached the lumberyard, I suddenly remembered I had forgotten my lunch. I decided to leave my stuff under a lumber pile because there was no sense taking that back with me. I looked around to see that no one was watching. I wanted to be certain that no one would steal my fishing equipment, especially my tackle box, being that it was my dearest possession. I just knew that the first thing any thief would want would be my red and white Daredevil.

When I pushed my equipment under the lumber pile, I felt some snow and ice. I had uncovered a chunk of ice that had not yet melted from winter. I cracked a piece for myself and picked away the dirt and sawdust. I felt sure that I would have a great day, being that I was already eating my dessert.

I trudged back to the house to get my peanut butter and jelly sandwiches. The night before they looked pretty awful to me after just having had supper. I had made three. After making the first one, I nearly hadn't made any more. By now I was beginning to cuss myself for not having made five sandwiches because I was really hungry!

I slipped into the house. Everyone was still asleep. I could hear my dad "sawing wood" in the bedroom.

I looked under my cot, and, sure enough, my brown paper sack was there with my peanut butter and jelly sandwiches packed inside. I ate one sandwich while I thought of my exciting day ahead of me. The peanut butter stuck to the roof of my mouth but it was good. I stopped for a drink from the water pail. Some of the bread from my mouth was still in the dipper when I finished. I put the dipper back in the pail and watched the crumbs float around the top of the water, then sink slowly to the bottom. I knew my mother would be upset if she had witnessed that little scene, and I wished I had been more thoughtful.

As I walked out of the house, I was careful not to let the screen door slam. I ran swiftly down our dirt street toward the lumberyard. As I ran, I darted and faked, making football gestures with my body like a halfback. I must have scored at least five touchdowns before I crossed the railroad tracks. I now had a good view of Dickinson's Lumberyard.

The lumbermen were starting to come out into the yards, so it had to be about 7:00 a.m. I knew I had to act fast or the lumberyard watchman would catch me and run me out of there. "Maybe one of the lumbermen has already found my pole and tackle box," I thought to myself. All my previous joys turned to a feeling of fright. I sneaked down a row of piles, and I could plainly see my gear under the pile where I had left it. I was really happy that it was undisturbed. I quickly managed to get everything in my arms, and then I ran straight for the railroad tracks. I knew that the watchman would have no authority over me while I was on the tracks.

As I walked down the tracks, I could hear the waves from Lake Irving hitting the shore. I was in love with that beautiful lake. I promised myself that some day when I got big I would own a cozy cabin, a speedboat, plenty of fishing equipment, and a big dock. Most of all, I'd be very, very rich.

I was headed for the Mississippi River that connected Lake Irving and Lake Bemidji. The river was about a half-mile long. When you stood on the riverbank, you could see either lake from your right or left. There were a total of five bridges that crossed the river and I knew each by heart. The first bridge was the new bridge where the cars and trucks crossed. There was no fishing from on top of that bridge, but one could stand underneath and fish. Around and under the new bridge one could catch nice walleyes, but that required using minnows for bait and a good casting rod and reel. Minnows cost money and so did the rod and reel, so I never fished there. At least once a year my dad fished there, and he would let me use his rod and reel while he rested or ate his lunch. The second bridge was the Old Highway Bridge. It was used when the old highway was the only road into town. It was crumbly and nearly worn out. You could fish from that bridge if you wanted to, but there was nothing there as this was the shallow part of the river. There was also so much junk at the bottom of the river at that spot causing snags, which meant you would break your line and lose your hooks. I couldn't afford that so I seldom if ever gave that area a try.

The next three bridges were railroad bridges, and they were the best for sun fishing and also climbing. There wasn't one part of those bridges I didn't know. You could crawl all over them. There were places where you could crawl underneath the tracks and get within twelve inches from the bottom of an entire train. That was a great feeling to be about one foot below a big steam locomotive and still know that nothing would happen to you. Sometimes hot water would fall on your arms, or a cinder would drop on your face, but who cared. When you were really cold, a good way to get warmed up was by lying below a steam engine. It was especially great when the steam engine was just holding there for an hour or so. Every three minutes, while it was in holding, the big black engine would make a very loud "haaaaaarrummmph." A big cloud of dark smoke would then come from the smokestack. Then it would release a cloud of steam from its sides making a hissing sound. "Haaarrumph, sssssttt, haaarrumphh, sssssst", it would beller and squeal as it waited for the engineer to squeeze the right levers.

The railroad bridges had pilings all around them. The pilings were creosote treated poles that were pounded down into the river bottom. They were placed in front of the bridges so that the ice would not take the bridge out in the spring. Generally they stuck out of the water by about a foot or so. One thing was for sure, the sunfish liked being around those pilings; and it was just about the most fun to jump from piling to piling loaded with my fishing equipment, lunch and all, and then sit on top of one of the pilings all by myself and fish.

I knew those pilings by heart, so it wasn't hard for me to jump to the furthest one out in the river. In seconds, my cork was nestled nicely on the top of the water with my hook threaded with angleworms teasing every sunfish in the area. About the greatest thrill was to watch that cork quiver, bounce around, move a little to the left and then to the right, and then snap! under it would go.

I hadn't been perched on the piling long before I had caught six really nice sunnies. They were strung on my stringer and tied to the piling. I had about four big worms left and decided to put them all on my hook before I headed for home. Once I lost them, I knew that I would be done for the day.

I dropped my line as far out into the water as I could. I didn't have to wait for more than three seconds before my cork went down. I pulled back on my pole, and as I did so, it felt like I had hooked into a log. So I slid the pole down to the water to unhook the snag, when all of a sudden, something on the other end nearly pulled my pole right out of my hand. My heart started beating madly, for I thought that maybe I had some kind of a big fish on my line.

I managed to pry the big thing toward the piling; and, in doing so, it made a direct charge toward me causing me to lose my balance and fall into the water. I immediately dog-paddled to shore. When I got to the bank, I looked out into the river to find my pole. I saw just the end of it sticking up right in the middle of the river. It seemed to be heading in the direction of Lake Irving. I ran up to the Northern Pacific Bridge; but by the time I got there, the pole was moving toward the Great Northern Bridge. Every once in a while it would come up and rest on the top of the water and then down it would go again. It was well past the Great Northern Bridge headed toward the Soo Line Bridge when I decided to follow it alongside the bank. I followed it as it went under the Soo Line Bridge and could plainly see it was definitely headed toward Lake Irving; and at the rate it was going, in minutes it would be well out into the lake.

I ran like wildfire for a tiny dock that extended about five feet from the bank of the river. I knew it was my last chance. As I got out on the dock, I looked down in the water but my pole was nowhere to be seen. I waited for what seemed like an hour, and then over by some reeds on the side of the riverbank my yellow bamboo pole slowly surfaced. I ran to the bank as fast as I could. As I approached the reeds, I could see that I would easily be able to get ahold of the end of my pole. Just as I was about to grab my pole, I looked out into the river. About twenty feet from the bank I could see the biggest fish I had ever seen. It truly looked larger than any that were ever entered in the fish contest down at the sporting goods store. It was a big Northern Pike. I could see that it had my hook in its mouth!

I got ahold of the pole and ran to the top of the bank as fast as I could run, never looking behind me. I pulled like I had never pulled before. When I reached the top of the hill, I turned around to see if the fish was still on my hook.

There it was, flopping in the sand on the shore, and in seconds I was standing right beside him. He was mine, all mine! Boy, oh boy, he was a lunker!

As I stood there looking at him, I was very confident. Then all of a sudden he made a big flop, and I noticed he was no longer hooked; he had gotten the hook loose from his mouth! He started bouncing down toward the water. I dashed down the bank to stop him. He began thrashing around, throwing sand in my face. Finally about five feet from the water's edge I had him. Like a wrestler, I had my whole body over the top of him. I laid on top of him until he quit flopping. When I finally felt that he was motionless, I hooked him again with my line and pulled him back up the bank. He was dead all right, and he was going nowhere. I put him back into the water to wash him off and then laid him in the grass.

I took my jackknife out and began cutting a big crotch from a willow tree. While I was making the cut, I watched my big fish lie there in the hot sun. He was deader than a doornail, and I began to feel good inside, like I had never felt before. I finally cut my carrying stick and slipped one end through his gills and out his mouth. I put him over my back and started back for my tackle box and my other fish. This was the first time I had ever left my tackle box for such a long time and that began to worry me. As I approached the spot where I had left it, I could see my little box perched on the top of the piling just as it was when I had hooked into the big fish. I left my fish on the bank while I worked my way out to the piling. I grabbed my box and my sunfish and came back to the bank feeling better than ever.

I started for home with all my gear and my big fish. I was so happy and excited I could hardly wait to see my mother's eyes. I stopped at least fifteen times to look at that big lunker; and he was, without a doubt, the biggest fish I had ever seen. And I had seen lots of them down at the sporting goods store. I ran at a full gait the last half of the way home.

When I came trotting up to the house, I had at least ten younger kids following me. Even the neighbors were outside on the porches looking at me. How proud I was! I felt like I was Mayor Anderson leading the Fourth of July parade.

My mother and father were raking the yard. They were watching me as I came into the yard. My dad lifted the big fish from my shoulder saying, "Holy smokes, that's the biggest Northern Pike I have seen in a long, long time." My body began to tingle; I was so happy and proud I wanted to cry.

My dad said, "We're going to enter that big horse." My mom told me to get cleaned up quickly so that I could go with my dad. I hadn't imagined that all of this would turn out so good. I ran to the house as fast as I could to get ready to go downtown.

Imagine me, going downtown right into the sporting goods store with that fish! Imagine me, going downtown especially because of the fish and with my dad driving the car! "My Lord," I thought, "many times we all had to walk to and from church in order to save on the gas! Boy, my dad must surely think this is a pretty important deal!"

CHAPTER 5
"Well, I'll be Danged!"

When I came out of the house all cleaned up and ready to go with my dad, I found a good-sized crowd had gathered. Faye and George Nelson, the Bergstroms, and even the Hardings were there. I saw Nancy and Patty Wiggs both eating a peanut butter sandwich. Joyce Edwards, my special girlfriend, was waiting, too. I felt kind of embarrassed being in front of all those people. Then Wally came up to me with the biggest smile I had ever seen on him. He said, "Boy, Billy, that's a big fish. Where did you get him?"

I began to tell Wally the whole story when my father said, "Well, Bill, let's go."

"Bill," I thought to myself--"Bill." My father had never called me "Bill" before. Boy, was that something-- "Bill!" Goose pimples started running down my back and ran clean to my legs. I couldn't talk, as I didn't know what to say. My dad was too nice!

We got into our 1931 Chevrolet, fish and all, and proceeded to go to town. We were one of the few families who owned a car in Mill Park. I was very, very proud when we backed our black Chevy out of the driveway and onto the street.

As we started up the street, my father said, "Now, tell me all about it, Billy; tell me how you caught that big fish." I started to think. I knew my dad had forbidden my going to the tracks, and he never would have sanctioned my sitting on those pilings. I knew I had to lie. I had to tell a different story from what I had experienced, and I had to make it good.

I said that I was fishing from Locken's dock on Lake Irving, just fishing there for small sunfish, when all of a sudden that big fish hit my worm. "He pulled the pole right out of my hand and got all tangled up in the weeds. I watched him fight and struggle for a long time," I said. "When he came closer to the dock, I grabbed the pole. I then ran straight for the shore and I had him."

My dad said, "Well, I'll be danged. I never would have thought there would be a fish that size that would come so close to the shore."

As we drove toward town, all my father could say was, "Well, I'll be danged!" I knew that this meant he was puzzled about my story. I had plenty more to tell him should he ask; but he never did say any more except, "Well, I'll be danged!"

As we came near town, we began to pass by the river; and I could see the Northern Pacific Bridge as we passed over the Old Highway Bridge. As I looked down toward the bank, I could see my lunch sack on the shore. I knew it had one peanut butter sandwich in it. And there was my piling that I had sat on all morning. There wasn't a soul around. I was the only one who really knew the true story.

We came closer to town, turned left on Main Street and drove right up in front of the sporting goods store. Parked near our car were a great many newer cars with Iowa, Illinois, and Nebraska license plates.

My dad pulled the big Northern from the back part of the floor of the car, and we walked into the store together. I don't know who was the prouder, my dad or me. When we came up to the man behind the counter, he said, "What the heck have you got there, Hank, a whale?" I didn't know my dad knew this man; and for that reason, I was glad that I had never done any fooling around by his store.

The man took the fish from my dad and placed it on his scale. "Wow," he said, "this Northern weighs eighteen pounds, six and one-half ounces." I knew that had to be a lot because I had only weighed seventy-three pounds when I left school in the spring.

The man then took a big white card and began filling in the blanks. "Let's see," he said, "eighteen pounds, six and one-half ounces. Where'd you catch him, Hank?"

My dad said, "I didn't catch him. My son here did."

Then the man smiled and said, "Tell me about how you caught him, Son." I started to choke up. I hesitated for what seemed to be the longest time. Would I be able to tell the story the way that I had told it to my dad just a few minutes ago? Surely I'd leave something out; then he would know for sure I was lying to him.

My dad said, "Well, I was with him and he seems a little shy and excited about it right now. So I'll tell you how it happened." I couldn't believe it! My dad was saving me from lying to him and he was lying right back on top of it!

"Well, you see," said my dad, "we got up fairly early this morning, and Bill and I went out on Lake Irving, you know, where Smith's Bar is? Well, we were drifting over that bar with minnows on, and all of a sudden Bill's pole went down. We struggled with that fish for over an hour. He sashayed back and forth, back and forth, and finally I netted him for Billy here. Right, Son?"

I, of course, said, "Yes, Dad, that's exactly the way it happened."

"Well, I'll be danged," said the store man, "I'll be danged."

My dad looked at me and winked. He had never done that before; and I never knew him to lie, but as long as he was happy so was I.

The man told us that there was a good chance for me to win the monthly prize that would be $5 in trade. "The yearly prize is an outboard motor, but someone has already beat you out of that by three pounds," he said. "But you still have a chance for second prize for the year which is this rod and reel."

By now I was breathless. I looked at that rod and reel. It was so clean and neat. The reel was the prettiest silver I had ever seen. It was a level winder! It had a beautiful pearl handle. The rod had a cork handle, and it felt so good to put that rod in my hands that I didn't want to give it up.

I said a prayer right then and there, "Please, God, let me win this rod and reel, as there isn't anyone who I know of that wants it more." Just then I thought of the lie I told my dad and I was sick. "God will never honor my prayer for telling that lie," I thought to myself. I said three Hail Marys quickly, hoping to redeem myself.

I decided right then and there that I would tell my dad the truth when I got to the car. When we left the store, I wasn't as happy as I had been when we had come in. I knew I would feel better when I had told my dad the real story. All the way home my dad talked and talked about the big fish. I didn't have a chance to open my mouth.

When we arrived at home, my mother had supper all ready. My sisters were at the table and everyone was waiting for us. My father told everything to my mother and sisters, even how he had changed the story. After supper, I left the table and went out into the woodshed. I piled a whole lot of wood while I thought about how I was going to tell the right story to my dad. I finally got up enough courage. I came directly into the house and said, "Dad?"

My mother said, "He's gone fishing down on Locken's Dock."

I ran out of the house and down to the tracks. I sat on the bank, and sure enough there on Locken's Dock was my father casting his rod and reel for all he was worth. I knew he didn't stand a chance.

The tears came to my eyes. I felt badly that he was down there wasting his time. I had lied to him. I was so sorry that I had gone fishing and caught that big fish. The more I thought about it, the more the tears streamed down my face. Finally I got up and walked slowly toward home.

CHAPTER 6
"Pioneer, Bemidji Pioneer!"

Every time I went downtown, I checked on the fishing contest. My big Northern held up and I won the rod and reel! I told my dad that it was all his and that I would take his old one. He said we'd see. We nailed them up on the wall in the basement stairway. My bamboo pole was placed between the two rods and reels. It was some sight to see as one walked down the basement stairs. My dad and I were very proud of our fishing equipment.

The rest of the summer was pretty uneventful. I don't think I received over three or four lickings. The trips to the woodshed were for not weeding the garden like I should have or my having neglected to get the wood in--just stupid things when I should have known better.

One day I was wrestling with my sister Lois who constantly fought with me. I backed her up against the front room window; and, in the process, we knocked over the ice sign that was sitting on the windowsill. When I put the sign back in the window, I put the wrong side up, causing the ice man to bring in 25 pounds instead of the usual 15 pound block. Because of this there was little room all week for the milk and butter. On top of that, the next day I forgot to remove the water tray from underneath the icebox; and, of course, the water overflowed onto the floor. By the time we noticed it, the water had sat long enough to curl up the linoleum. After that, every time my father was irritable, he would cast his eyes on that curled-up spot on the floor and tell how the whole house was going to fall to pieces because I didn't watch things and do my jobs. It seemed like I couldn't do the right thing no matter how hard I tried.

I guess when I left the house that particular morning, I knew before I started that it was going to be another bad day. I made myself a thick, creamy peanut butter sandwich and went out on the woodpile to eat it. I decided to stay home.

All of a sudden little rocks started flying off to my side, and I knew that Wally was somewhere close by. The rocks were glancing off the creosote ties that were piled by my father for fall sawing. We heated our house with those ties each winter. They were old castoffs that the railroad would burn or throw away, but the section men got first chance at them. My dad was first to get the ties because he was the first man in rank after the section foreman. The section foreman didn't want them because, as my father said, "He didn't have any kids to feed and he was a lot richer than we were." He burned coal in his heater. My dad always said that some day he would be a section foreman and then we would have things a lot better, too. I prayed every night my dad would get to be a section foreman; and then when he was boss, we would burn coal and I wouldn't have to pile that wood. One of the reasons why the section foreman burned coal was because he knew the depot agent well, and a pail or two of coal a week was a fringe benefit just like the ties were an extra compensation for the first man.

Suddenly Wally was standing right in front of me and proposed that we go to work and make ourselves a little money. This idea made me feel excited, for the only job I ever had was picking acorns in our front yard and from any other oak tree I could find. Every time Lois, Pat and I had a sugar sack full, we would take them all the way across town to the zoo. We were paid a penny a pound for the acorns, and you could make some pretty good money if you worked at it. One year I made enough money to buy myself a short-sleeved striped shirt that I thought the world of. I wore that shirt for what seemed like all my life.

"You bet I'm interested in making some money, Wally. What are we going to do, pick scrap iron?" I asked. Scrap iron picking wasn't all that bad, especially if you could throw in a few railroad spikes, plates or angle irons. Railroad iron really made the weight count up, but the guy who bought our iron wouldn't always take the railroad iron, as the railroad company would really raise cane if they caught you stealing any of their iron. Besides, if my dad ever knew I stole scrap from the railroad, he would really take me to the woodshed.

Wally said, "No, not picking scrap iron, we're going to sell newspapers."

"Newspapers," I said. "You can't get a route up here on the hill. Who would buy a paper?" The only people who bought a paper that I knew about were the Malleys, and they got their paper from a kid in Nymore.

"No, not that route stuff," said Wally. "We'll sell on the streets. All we need is six cents apiece. We go to the Pioneer office, buy three papers at two cents apiece and sell them for a nickel each. We keep the three cents for each paper we sell."

"Wow, me selling papers on the street," I uttered. I had always wanted to be in business like that for myself. I would like to have had a route but never knew how to get one. Imagine me standing on the corner yelling, "Bemidji Pioneer", as loud as I could. "Why, I could sell maybe a hundred a night," I thought. I quickly figured out that a hundred a night would give me three dollars a day, twenty-one dollars a week. Geez, I'd be rich in one month!

We started down the sidewalk when Wally brought up the fact that we still needed some money to start with and that he had gone through the whole house and couldn't scrape up one red cent. So the next move was mine. I went back into our house. I went through my mother's purse. She had a fifty-cent piece, several buttons, and a safety pin in her coin purse. I didn't dare take that fifty-cent piece because she would miss that without question. I just knew our business venture was over, but then I remembered my dad's coin collection. I went into my parents' bedroom, opened the top drawer of their chest of drawers and there was the cigar box where he kept his valuables and his coins.

Inside the box was a worn railroad envelope that contained lots of pennies. My dad collected Indian head pennies. There must have been sixty or seventy of them. I took twelve of them, six for Wally and six for me. As I was about to close the box, I decided to take two more for candy.

I had never thought of my father's collection before and felt kind of good to know I had a steady source of money for emergencies just like this.

When I got outside, Wally was waiting patiently and quickly asked me if I had found any money. I said, "Yes, I got fourteen cents; and when we need more, I know where we can get it." I knew Wally was proud of me, and I knew that getting that money made me more of a special friend of his. At the same time, I thought about my father's collection and how proud he was of it. I believed that there would be no problem because, as soon as I made three dollars, I'd slip back the fourteen cents and no one would know the difference. We would all be happy.

We went downtown kicking sticker bushes with our bare feet. That was a real sign of toughness; and even though it hurt a lot, I could kick sticker bushes as well as Wally. In fact, I could stand right in the middle of them and dance, and he couldn't even do that. Sometimes Wally would say, "Go dance on a sticker bush," and I'd do just that. It hurt, but I would really laugh about it. Wally found it unbelievable that I could stand the pain.

We passed Dickinson's Lumberyard, the stockyards, and it wasn't but a few minutes until the bridges were in sight. We shot at least fifty rocks at the bridge and pilings and were having a fine time just drifting along headed in the direction of the Pioneer newspaper office.

As we started into town, we detoured in the back way. The railroad tracks were branching into the various storage buildings and here and there were boxcars being unloaded by men at work. We watched three men unload a good-sized tractor. They almost tipped it off the car when they were coming down the ramp with it. It would have been some sight had they put that red tractor off on its back just to see it break into pieces, but it didn't happen.

Wally was ahead of me by about one hundred yards when he started waving to me in a motion that meant come in a hurry. Obviously he had found something exciting and interesting. I ran quickly toward him to find out what he had discovered.

By the time I got to Wally, he had pulled himself up and into a boxcar. Wally said, "Come on up; you can't believe what all is in here." I climbed up and Wally helped me in. It smelled so good inside that I wanted to smell and save that aroma forever. There were many boxes of bananas--lots of them; more bananas than I had ever seen in my life. On a pile of the boxes of bananas were stacks and stacks of coconuts all wrapped up resting in straw nests. Then over in another pile was a stack of peaches and pears. The boxcar contained a treasure chest of fruit, the likes of which I had never in my life seen before.

By this time, Wally was eating a banana and he had a whole bunch in his hand. His mouth was so full of bananas that you could just make out a smile on his tan face. He handed me a bunch and then grabbed another bunch for himself at the same time.

I ate about seven bananas before I felt a smack on the back of my neck. It was the strangest feeling I had ever had. I turned around and it was Wally again. He had peeled a banana and squeezed it all over my back. I immediately ran after him and tried to squeeze a banana in his hair. We started to throw the bananas at each other, and it wasn't long until we had a banana fight. We used them as pistols; we made ourselves look like bulls and bullfighters. We squeezed them in our hands and put them in our mouths, making them real watery; then we blew them out through our teeth. I never had so much fun in my life!

All of a sudden we heard a noise on the top of the boxcar. We both stopped, and in one motion jumped out of the boxcar and ran like the dickens. We ran for at least four blocks, down through an old junkyard and behind the creamery. When we reached the back of Ching's Restaurant, we walked up the alley alongside the building, gasping for breath. We sat perched up against Ching's building for at least 15 minutes with our faces headed right into the exhaust fan of old Ching's cafe. We continued gasping for breath and Ching's cooking air was all we could get. I knew I would never be able to eat bananas or any type of Chinese cooking again.

We rested there for quite some time and finally decided there were no railroad bulls around. We tiptoed out onto the sidewalk and saw that not two blocks away was the Bemidji Pioneer office. I was glad to see it because I knew that better things were ahead for us.

We weren't in there but two minutes and out we came with three papers each. It was hard to believe that we were in business so fast. I no more than turned around when a big, fat man dressed in a brown suit said, "Hey, kid, is that the Pioneer?"

I said, "Yes, sir, it sure is."

He said, "Gimme one."

I handed him the paper, and he gave me a nickel. I looked at Wally and said, "This sure enough is easy." That warm nickel really heated my hand up!

I immediately marched right back into the Pioneer office, put six cents on the table, and said, "Give me three more." I left the store with a total of five Pioneers and I felt darned proud. I was probably carrying more papers than any other kid on the street. I had it all figured out; I would sell these papers for a quarter, be back at home with my father's fourteen Indian heads, and that would leave me eleven cents. With Wally's six cents he owed me, I would have seventeen cents. I decided in my mind that Wally could have that six cents. After all, it was his idea. "Besides," I thought, "he'd really like me a lot better for it."

There I was on the corner of Third Street and Beltrami Avenue. I started hollering as loud as I could, "Bemidji Pioneer! Bemidji Pioneer!" I yelled so loud that everyone within five blocks could hear me. People came by and snickered at me. One woman commented to the other that I was some sight, standing in those blue, holey bib overalls, no shirt, no shoes and yelling my head off.

I stood on that corner for at least two hours, and I never sold one lousy paper! I began to get a little worried. As a result, I started wandering from the corner. I turned off Beltrami Avenue and went by St. John's Ice Cream Shop. I saw a much smaller kid coming up the sidewalk. He had nice clothes on, the kind I never had. I was sure he was headed for St. John's Store to get himself an ice cream cone. He was obviously younger than me by at least a year or so. I couldn't stand his getup; and it made me mad to think that he was going to buy an ice cream cone, and all of my money was invested in my papers.

As he came by me, I asked him if he wanted to buy a paper.

He said, "No thanks."

I said, "Have you got money to buy yourself some ice cream?"

He replied, "Yes."

"Well, then you've got money to buy a paper, too!"

He said, "My parents get the paper at home."

"Don't give me your sob story, kid. Get your money out because you're going to buy one of these papers. And if you don't buy one pretty quick, you'll end up with two."

As far as I could see, his parents weren't around; but for that matter, neither was Wally. A shot ran through my mind; maybe he had a bigger brother or something. I began to get a little worried. About that time he started to dart into St. John's, and I caught him by the back of his neck and pulled him back onto the sidewalk.

In the scuffle I dropped my newspapers, but I had him by the shoulders with both of my hands. He seemed so light and easy to handle. I was surprised and proud of the power I had. I didn't realize I was so strong. I started to shove him around and kept saying, "Are you going to buy a paper or not?"

44

He kept saying, "NO!"

I knew that pretty soon people would start coming around, and he was obviously in the right and I was in the wrong. I needed to end this confrontation quickly, but really didn't know how. I decided to give him one last push and that would be the end of it. I took my hand and grabbed him by his hair, tossing his head against St. John's glass front door. As I pushed him, his head went right through the glass. It made a perfect hole. In one continuous motion, I pulled back on his hair; and his head came forward, out of the hole. Just then the top part of the glass came down across the hole like a guillotine, just missing its mark. There was blood all over my hand and on his head. I looked down at my papers and they had red blotches all over them.

Just then the store owner came out, leaped to my side, and started hollering at both of us raving that we had broken his window, and that it was going to cost, "Maybe $50." By then a crowd had gathered around us. They were all staring and talking about the whole affair. I looked around and there was Victor Paulis in his big, blue policeman's uniform. He looked so mean and stern. I wanted to run away, but I knew there was no use. I was in deep, bad trouble, and all I could see was the vision of my father's face just before we went to the woodshed.

CHAPTER 7
Red Wing for Sure

We were both transported to the hospital in the storeowner's car. My hand was cut some but no worse than what I had done many times with my jackknife. The other boy had cuts around his neck but not really deep cuts. His situation did not seem to be much worse than mine. We both were covered with bandages and that made it look much worse than it actually was.

But, as I sat in the doctor's office, the whole problem was getting worse by the minute. First, how would I explain the money for the papers? Would the spree with the bananas in the boxcar come out? How much would the window cost? What would the police do? How much would the hospital cost? And would this kid really be okay? And the real big problems were how mad would my dad be, how many lickings would he give me, or just what would he do with this terrible, bad situation. It was worse than anything I had ever done. No punishment could possibly be bad enough. I could not even cry. I was never so afraid in all my life. I began to pray. I said Hail Marys and Our Fathers, even the Glory Be to the Fathers, which I usually skipped. I prayed slowly, then fast. Then I would think about my father, the bandaged kid, then the money, then the Indian heads, and then the bananas. It just would not quit; the whole thing kept going around and around in my mind. I wished I were dead!

The nurse then took me back to the hospital waiting room. She asked, "What is your parent's name?"

I told her, "Henry Kirtland, but he is working now." I looked out through the hospital waiting room and it was dark. "Oh, my God," I thought to myself. "It is dark and I am not home yet, and I did not get my wood box filled. I have never been in worse trouble."

"What's your telephone number, Son?" the nurse asked.

She was so nice. I did not deserve to be treated nicely; didn't she know that? "Seven, three seven W," I said, and I knew the time was getting closer and closer when I would have to face the music.

I thought of Sister Louise. She used to say, "Make sure you tell the truth, the whole truth. Make sure you tell the truth."

I began to try to get my story ready. Should I bring up the bananas? How about the Indian head pennies? I would have to tell about that; where else would I have gotten the money? Besides, Wally would be asked his side of the story. Would Wally tell the truth? Would I get him into trouble? "He is the least of my worries," I said to myself. I decided I would tell the whole story. There would be no holding back. I would tell the whole thing and probably get killed, but that is the way it would be.

The hospital door opened and there was my mother. She was first. She came toward me with big tears in her eyes. She grabbed me and hugged me; I could not believe it, and I knew I did not deserve to be treated that way. I just felt so ashamed and guilty. Then while my mother was hugging me, I looked behind her and there was my dad. He looked meaner than I had ever seen him. My mom and dad talked briefly with the nurse. Then, he said, "Let's go." He grabbed me by the hand and out we went. He did not say another word, but I could tell by the way he squeezed my hand that I was really in for it.

We went straight for our '31 Chevy. He opened the door on his side for me. He tipped the seat forward and that was my cue. I started to get in and as I did, he slapped my backside with his open hand. It did not hurt at all, but I started to cry and make my usual moaning sounds.

We drove faster than I had ever ridden in our car. My father was always a very careful, slow driver, but not tonight. We came to a stop sign that was on a quiet residential street. My dad turned around and said, "What am I going to do with you?"

I squealed, "I don't know."

He cracked me about three or four times. I started to lean into the back corner of the car seat but then decided that I should take my medicine. I moved right near to him so he could get some good whacks at me. He hit me on the head and shoulders; and one of his slaps rang my ears so badly, I didn't think I would hear again. My mother began to cry and it was truly a bad, bad scene.

My dad shouted, "Can't you be good? Can't you be good? Will you be good? When will you be good?"

And all the time he kept banging away at me. I sobbed like I had never sobbed before. I was not crying because of my hits; they did not hurt anymore. I was crying because it seemed my father was out of his head, my mother was terribly upset, and I was the cause of it all. I now knew I brought nothing but grief to these poor people.

Then my father did not say a thing. He just drove. My mother did not talk either; she just sat there sniffling.

I said, "Dad, from now on I promise you I will be good."

And then my dad began to cry, too. I had never seen him act like this. He was sobbing and swearing and saying, "What am I going to do with you?"

I kept answering, "I will be good; I promise I will be good."

I could finally see our house. We drove up into the yard rapidly. The sudden braking of the car made us all lurch forward.

I made a beeline for the house and my father was right behind me. He swatted me once on the backside, and I was knocked against the side of the house. He opened the screen door, motioned me in, and whacked me a good one as I entered the house. I did not really know what to do once I got inside, so I just stood by the kitchen table.

The table was set. Cold sauerkraut and wieners were in their respective dishes, and it was obvious no one had eaten.

I had fouled that up, too. Our entire supper was all shriveled up. None of it looked appetizing.

My dad ordered me to sit down and tell the whole story. It seemed he knew a lot more about it than I thought, so I proceeded to outline in detail the story beginning with my sitting on the woodpile.

Throughout the entire story my dad would roll one cigarette right after another. I knew he was terribly upset, as he spilled so much tobacco from his Bull Durham sack. Usually he was so very careful about that. There were times when he would roll his cigarettes over the newspaper so that he could salvage all of the spillings. But not tonight; he was careless and unconcerned about wasted tobacco.

When I finished the story, he kept pumping me as to whether or not I had told it all. I was very relieved and, yet, felt like maybe he had not thought it so bad after all.

He then began to lay out my punishment. He said that my college money in the bank from the railroad accident was going to have to be taken for repayment of the bananas and the window at St. John's. He repeatedly asked me how I thought I was going to like it in the Red Wing Reform School.

"Reform school?" I asked. I began to moan and squeal, and then my mother started crying worse than ever.

My father said he supposed that the doctor bills would run very high and the likelihood was good that the boy's parents would probably sue us. "Are you ready to give up this house, Margaret?" he asked. "And our car and saw rig and all of our property? You see what this kid has done to us?"

God, I felt so bad, but there wasn't a thing I could do. There was no way out, except to just sit there on the stool. We stayed up very late that night planning out what we were going to do. In the meantime, my father made several telephone calls. One of them was to the boy's parents and the other was to the yardmaster of the railroad.

He came back into the kitchen suggesting that the chances were pretty good that he would lose his job and the parents were going to start some suit charges, probably in the morning. He said that we were going to go downtown tomorrow morning and report everything to Victor Paulis at the police station.

Finally we went to bed. I sobbed nearly all night; I was so frightened. I prayed myself to sleep, hoping that I would never wake up again.

But morning did come. I could not eat a thing. My father did not eat either. He just smoked and smoked. He said that we would be leaving for the police station shortly. I tried to cry but no tears would come. I was cried out. I began to think what it would be like in the Red Wing Reform School, nothing but bread and water and pounding rocks all day long. I visualized myself in a striped suit and all the mean guys scaring me. I wondered what my cell partner would be like. Finally, I was able to cry again.

We stopped at St. John's Ice Cream Shop and paid for the window. It cost $78.

My dad and I parked in front of the police station. He told me that if we parked there longer than fifteen minutes that Victor Paulis would come out to get me and throw me in jail. I vowed over and over again that this would be the last of it, that never again would I get into trouble like that. Finally after fourteen minutes, my dad backed out of the police station parking lot and headed for home. I wanted to sing or whistle to express my happiness, but, of course, didn't dare.

The parents of the boy I had pushed through the window covered their own hospital costs. They never sued us. My dad didn't get fired from his job.

My dad's railroad insurance policies covered my hospital costs. Knowledge of all of this came to me over the years as I never asked about any of the details, and my dad never offered to discuss them. I always felt it better to leave well enough alone.

CHAPTER 8
Salve Business

As the weeks rolled by slowly but surely, the trouble I had caused was mentioned less and less. I was happy for that. It wasn't long before I began to stray away from the yard. One day I went down past Bergstrom's. I shot one swallow from the electric wire. I had a good feeling that things were going to get back to normal again.

I strolled in behind Edward's house and began walking back home by the bank between our house and the railroad tracks. While walking along, I pulled sprigs of timothy to chew and spotted a piece of mail that was not yet opened. The address on the envelope was blurred so that I could not read it. I opened the envelope in hopes that there would be a lot of money. Inside the envelope was a colored shiny sheet of paper. In very large letters it said:

HEY KIDS!
EARN MONEY,
SELL CLOVERINE SALVE

No Money Down. Just fill out this blank and receive ten boxes of Cloverine Salve along with ten beautiful pictures. Sell each box for 25¢ and keep 10¢ per box or earn points toward these valuable premiums.

In the middle of the premium list was a picture of a very beautiful red bike. It had a carrier on the back, whitewall tires, saddlebags, a light on the front fender, and a bell attached to the handlebars. There were pictures of other prizes, too--field glasses, microscopes, a chemistry set, Chinese checkers, regular checkers, and a Monopoly game.

I took the leaflet home and the bike kept flashing in my mind. I could see myself riding it downtown, saddlebags full of newspapers. I could visualize all of my friends gathered around looking at me on that bike; even Wally was there in disbelief. The colored slides kept popping in my mind and each was as exciting as the next.

In no time I was back at the house calling for my mother. We sat down and I showed her the bike and advertisement. My mother was dead set against the whole idea. She said, "We can't afford to buy the salve." I did everything I could to explain to her that we didn't have to buy it and they didn't charge for it. I told her, "I sell it, then send the money in; that's the way the whole thing works, Mom."

My mother said that we would have to wait until my dad came home to see what he thought. I could see that she was purposely trying not to be understanding or cooperative.

I went to my bedroom and looked at the pictures of the prizes again. The bike was so beautiful! Under the bike it said, "Sell only 100 orders and the bike is yours absolutely free." I knew I could sell Bergstrom's one and the Nelson's would be good for one, and surely Mr. Malley would buy one can and Joe MacMillan would be good for two or probably three cans, and I knew my mother would buy one or two and the Sisters at school; for sure, they would want a lot of that salve, and I could sell the salve on the streets. I was certain there would be no problem selling that salve!

I quickly multiplied 10 cans times 100 orders. My arithmetic came out that I would need to sell one million cans of salve. "That would be impossible," I thought. My hopes were shattered. "That can't be right," I said to myself. Then I thought I must have carried wrong or set my zeros up in the wrong columns. I figured the problem over and over. First I'd get 10,000, then 100,000, then 1,000, and finally I checked it enough times that I was sure that I only needed to sell 1,000 cans of Cloverine Salve to get that bike!

I was pretty sure that my father would give me the okay, so I began preparing my calling list. I wrote down the Bergstroms and Nelsons. I wrote the number of cans of salve beside each name. I went up and down the block in my mind and then placed their orders on paper. When I counted my total sales, I had 52. I subtracted 52 from 1,000 and had 948 cans to go. Before too long I had sold another five per day on the streets. Then I thought of my Grandma Schmit. "Old people need lots of salve," I said to myself, and then there was Aunt Dorothy, Uncle Fred, Aunt Vivian, and my other relatives. I was wishing I hadn't been so mean to my cousins at our last family reunion because that would no doubt hurt my sales to my aunts and uncles. Then I thought of the family reunion coming up. "Selling salve would be no problem at all," I sighed.

As I left the room, flashes of my red bike came back into my mind; and I got a grin on my face bigger than any I could remember in a long time. I looked in the frosted mirror hanging in my room. I said to myself, "Bill, you got yourself a bike! All you have to do is get your dad to give the okay." I smiled and winked at the reflection of a new businessman.

Then I realized I hadn't prepared my strategy with my dad. I had to get him ready, as he would never say yes unless everything was set. I wondered what kind of a mood he'd be in. Boy, I hoped he had had a good day! Then I said a short prayer, "Please, God, help him forget about the St. John's window."

I immediately went out to the woodshed and carried in two armloads of wood, filling the wood box to the brim. Then I went out in the yard and picked up all the paper I could find. It didn't take me but about ten minutes and I had the yard looking great. Not one piece of paper was in sight. I proceeded straight to the garden. Peas were my dad's favorite. I hoed three rows of peas. I then took our old cultivator and went through the entire garden. The black dirt was exposed throughout the entire area. It was beautiful! I ran for the house as fast as I could to check the icebox for water. The pan was half full, so I quickly emptied it. I then emptied the slop pail. It was nearly three-fourths full, and I quickly carried it out behind the toilet and dumped it high into the air.

Everything was falling into place. I went into my bedroom, made my bed, and straightened up my room. As I left the bedroom, I glanced at the mirror again. I was a mess; my face was dirty and sweaty and my hair was full of snarls. I had rooster tails in back, too. I knew all of that just might make a difference between yes or no to my venture. I quickly placed the wash pan on our wood stove and put several dippers of water in it. The pan started to jump a little on the stove; then the water began to collect tiny bubbles. I took two potholders and carried the wash pan over to the washstand. I then placed a clean washcloth in the pan and soaped it up real good. I scrubbed my face hard. I even washed the back of my neck. Usually I just hated this, but today I didn't mind at all; in fact, it felt pretty good. Some soap got into my eyes and that didn't even bother me. Then I thought maybe I should take a bath but decided against it, as it would take too much time to heat the water.

I wet my hair down with the leftover water in the wash pan, as it didn't seem to be that dirty. I took some of my dad's hair oil from the medicine cabinet and soaked my hair down with it. I then went to the mirror and combed my hair. I really looked nice. I knew that I would reach my goal and that my dad would give me the "go ahead" on the salve.

I went over to the corner by the icebox to sit down and wait for my dad. I sat in the highchair. It had the back sawed off; it was really a stool. It was the first thing my mother painted every spring. You always knew that spring was coming when my mother painted it. I checked to see if I had my leaflet in my pocket so I would be ready for my father's arrival. I sat in the highchair half-relaxed and confident, when I discovered that I had forgotten one more important thing, my dad's bedroom slippers! I ran quickly for my parents' bedroom and went straight to the closet. I was in such a hurry that after parting the curtain that partitioned off the closet, I tipped the night pot over onto the shoes that were on the floor. Pee ran all over the shoes and onto a couple of my dad's ties that had fallen from the coat hanger above. I didn't panic; I ran back to

54

the kitchen and grabbed three big rags from our rag drawer. They were rag leftovers from my dad's long winter underwear, and I knew they would pick up the pee like a sponge. I cleaned the mess up best as I could. With one last underwear leg, I squeezed my dad's two ties onto the rag and it made them fairly dry. I hung the ties back up on the coat hanger. Everything looked better than before. I spotted my dad's red furry bedroom slippers. My mother had bought them for my dad for Christmas. We were all very proud of them. I knew my dad would like the fact that I had thought to have his slippers ready as soon as he got home. He always took his boots off when he came into the house, placed his feet in the scrub pail, removed his shirt to his underwear shirt, sat at the kitchen table, and said, "Well, what's new, Margaret?"

"I'll even get the water ready for his feet," I thought. I now sat in the highchair with the leaflet about the Cloverine Salve in one hand, his bedroom slippers in the other, and the full scrub pail of rainwater under the highchair. I was almost fully prepared for his entrance. While I waited, I practiced my speech.

"Hi, Dad, how did work go today? Say, Dad, I have a thing here I would like you to do." That would be my first opening. I said to myself, "No, that was too fast. I'd better wait to see how his mood would be." I sure hoped that they hadn't put in ties because that was very hard work; and he never was in good spirits following a day of putting in ties.

Just then I heard the screen door slam and my heart began to thump. It was my father! He was home!

He entered the room with his black dinner pail in his one hand and his leather mitts in the other. He took one look at me. I was smiling and ready.

He asked, "What's wrong?"

I said, "Nothing."

"Why are you all cleaned up?" he asked.

"I don't know. I just wanted to do things right," I replied. "Did you see the yard?"

"Yeah," he said. "I can tell you picked up. Now what's wrong? What did you do?"

I asked him if he had had a chance to see the garden. "I weeded it, you know," I added. "Here, let me take your boots off, Dad, and let's soak your feet in this nice, warm rainwater here." I then led right into the project. "Say, Dad, have you ever heard of Cloverine Salve?"

He said, "No, I haven't."

I said, "Well, I've got a chance to sell Cloverine Salve. And Mom said she's all for my doing it if you will say it's okay." I could see my mom smiling while she was cutting potatoes for the frying pan. "I can earn a new bike if things go well; I can get some really good prizes besides the bike. And if I don't want to take the prizes after the bike, I can take the cash instead; and I'll be willing to give half of the cash to you and Mom. Maybe I can make enough so that we can buy Mom that fur coat we've always wanted to get her," I said, without taking a breath.

I showed my dad the colored leaflet and said, "It's all written down right here on this paper. What I want to do, Dad, is sell this Cloverine Salve for my extra work."

My dad took the brochure and started reading it. His lips always moved while he read and this time was no exception. I could see that he was really reading and concentrating on it, and again my heart started pounding. I had a good chance! I had to cinch it up somehow real quick! However, nothing would come to my mind. I needed to hit him really hard with something he would like. It seemed like ages before I managed to say, "Dad, you noticed that the yard looks really good, and the wood box is filled, and I did the garden like you always wanted. And you know what? All of that is something that I know can get done every day. I promise that if I could sell the salve so I can get the bike, those jobs would be done without my being asked. Not even once will you need to remind me. How about it, Dad? Do you think you feel like you can say yes to this salve business?" I pleaded.

My dad looked at me and smiled pleasantly and said, "Yes, I think it would be okay. You go ahead and make out the order and we'll send it in."

I grabbed my dad and hugged him so hard. As I looked over his shoulder, that beautiful red bike flashed back into my mind with me sitting on it just as big as you please. I pulled back and looked my dad square in the eyes and said, "Thanks, Dad, you won't be sorry about this."

For a moment I wondered if I had promised too much in the way of chores. Instantly that red bike flashed back into my mind, and I knew then that it would be worth the extra work.

CHAPTER 9
Lemonade Business

I filled the order out with my mother's help. It was a beautiful feeling to get that piece of important business accomplished. I personally placed it in the red iron mailbox out in front of our house, where everyone on the block put his mail. I had never had an occasion before to put my very own mail in that box; and when it dropped to the bottom, I knew that there was nothing in the world that could stop me from getting my bike.

The next day I waited for the mailman. I met him several blocks down our street and told him about my business venture, but most of all I wanted to know if my salve was on his truck. He told me that I would probably be looking at somewhere between two and three weeks for delivery. He also told me that he couldn't buy any salve because he was on duty and that both of us could go straight to jail if he were to talk about the salve while on duty. I was very disappointed, as I was counting on him for two boxes.

I could tell it was going to be a hot day, so I decided not to waste any more energy. It was going to be one of those really bad, boring days with nothing to do but sit around and be miserable. I knew that if I appealed to my mother for some ideas, she would come up with her same old answers. "You could fill your wood box and weed the garden. That'll keep you busy. Why don't you make yourself a thread and button whirler. You haven't done that in a long time. I know what would be perfect for you; why don't you go stick your head in the rain barrel, that'll cool you off." Then she would laugh about the whole ordeal. No matter what she said I would be unable to keep a sober face, eventually breaking into laughter.

I wished it were Saturday, because on each Saturday Lois and I usually went to the show. My mother would give us each a nickel, and we would walk to town and see a double feature western, a chapter of the current serial and two comedies.

The Elko Theater had a "Babes In Arms" policy. My sister would buy one ticket for herself, and I would wait for her by the main door. She would then carry me past the ticket taker. My sister had to really work very hard so that I would qualify as a Babe in Arms. I used to lock my arms around her neck and kind of limp along on one foot. Even though I was way too heavy for her, she never dropped me; our practice at home paid off.

Once we got past the ticket taker, we found two empty seats. I sat on her lap until the lights went out and the previews started. As soon as the serial began, everyone would cheer and jump up and down; that's when I would slip into my own seat.

When Lois decided it was time for us to really start living, she would begin distributing the candy kisses that we bought at the Hartz Store with our other nickel. Each candy kiss was individually wrapped. They contained peanut butter centers and were so darned good. Our bag of kisses always lasted us until the show was over. Sometimes we even had a few to eat on the way home.

For me, Saturdays were very special. I sure did wish it were Saturday.

I sat on my daybed thinking about what to do. "Maybe I should go fishing," I thought to myself. "Or I could go over to Blackbird Hill and go hunting." Then I remembered that my slingshot was broken. "That's it," I thought to myself, "I'll make a new slingshot." I remembered last year when I was down by the lake I had seen a willow crotch that was developing into a beautiful slingshot. Maybe by now it had grown and would be ready. Usually I was so much in a hurry to make a slingshot; but now with all this time on my hands, I could make one that would be really perfect.

I went to the kitchen to get the butcher knife. As I opened the icebox to get a chip of ice to suck on while going to the lake, I noticed that my mother had made a large container full of lemonade. I poured myself a glassful and it was so good and refreshing. As I drank the lemonade, I thought to myself, "Maybe I could make a little money if I set up my lemonade stand." That was better then making a new slingshot. Besides, the crotch probably hadn't grown much; and who knows, maybe I couldn't even find it.

I ran into my bedroom to get our card table. It was one of the nicest things we owned. We kept it in the cardboard case in which it had originally arrived. We had had that table for two years. It had a checker game painted in the center of it. It also had four silver ashtrays built into each corner of the table. I kept all of the money I made in one ashtray and the full pitcher of lemonade to be sold in one of the other ones.

Yes, I loved that card table, as it meant nothing but good times to us. My mom and dad always played whist with the Malleys on that table. My dad was in very good spirits and especially nice on those Saturday evenings when the Malleys came. Mr. Malley was my dad's supervisor on the railroad, and my dad made it very clear about our needing to stay on the good side of the Malleys. His job was the most important thing to all of us. My dad used to say, "When I'm out of work, we are out of food. I'll never go on relief." I could never really understand why he took that attitude, as some really nice people were on relief. I knew for a fact that the relief kids had the nicest cream-colored corduroy jackets, far nicer than the jacket that I wore. In fact, I used to get teased by those relief kids when I wore my frayed, old jacket.

When the Malleys would come to our house to play whist, I would stand behind my dad and watch him play. I knew that after all my experience of watching I could play better than any two of them put together. I watched closely. Then when my Grandma Schmit would come for the evening, my mom, dad, Grandma and I would play. I was my grandma's partner, and we never lost a game in our lives to my mom and dad. During the game my dad and Grandma would have a beer, and my mom and I would have a bottle of Royal Crown Cola. My grandma would always see to it that we had our beer and pop. Sometimes she even brought a jar of peanuts. We had plenty of meat sandwiches to eat after the game. God knows, when my grandma came, those were the nicest days of my life.

By this time I had the card table outside on the front lawn and my highchair behind it. I found my old sign in my box of treasures under my bed. I was really happy I had had enough sense to save that sign. The sign said, "Bill's lemonade 2¢ a glass." The "2" had been crossed out several times to be replaced by a "1." I quickly crossed out the "1" and made a "2" mark. I said to myself, "I'm not going down to one cent no matter what." I brought my crayons along just in case it became a long day.

I also took a handful of comic books, all of which I had read at least ten times. Mutt and Jeff, Scrooge McDuck and Amazon Lady were my favorites. I never let anyone watch me read Amazon Lady. I was always happy to see my sister Lois buy that comic so that I could read it. It was quite awhile before Lois realized I liked Amazon Lady; and until that happened, I could reap the benefits of her selection. When she finally found out that it was one of my favorites, she quit buying it for herself. She could be so darned ornery that way.

Finally I had the lemonade and several of my mother's finest glasses perched on the table ready for business.

As always, it looked as though my first customers would be Patty and Nancy Wiggs. They were good for a glass apiece. What made me mad was that I had to butter up to them before they would buy. Later they would tell Wally what I said, and I would have to lie out of it. Then I would have to go to confession. Every time I set up my lemonade stand it would mean a trip to Father Rawling's confession box. I would have to make one complete Act of Contrition until confession time. That's what I really hated, that darned lying to the Wiggs girls just to sell two lousy glasses of lemonade.

Today I decided I wasn't going to lie, no matter what. Sure enough, I had hardly sat down at the table when Nancy and Patty came out of their house from across the street. They watched me like a hawk and their grandma wasn't any better. I just hated to have to stay on their good sides, especially their grandma's, but she controlled the money.

They each came out with a peanut butter sandwich. Their sandwiches always looked so tasty and good, as their relief peanut butter was so creamy and ours was always so hard and sticky. Besides, they had bread right from the downtown bakery. Our bread was always homemade and it would tear apart easily. Their creamy peanut butter sandwiches on that slice of bought white bread always looked especially delicious to me.

I decided not to notice them. They looked like they had just come from a nap with their eyes all full of sleep and their dresses wrinkled. Both had long curls in their hair with a big ribbon on top of their heads. They were the homeliest girls, but they had the money.

"Whatcha doing?" Nancy asked.

"What does it look like?" I replied.

"You're selling lemonade, aren't you?" Patty said.

"How'd you guess?" I replied.

"How much is it?" they asked in harmony.

"You can read, can't you?" I suggested.

Patty said, "I'm going to ask Grandma for two cents so I can get a glass." While she ran back to the house, a good shiver went through my bones because that meant two "Guess-Whats" at the Nymore store.

Then Nancy said, "Let's not buy any lemonade from him. He's too crabby. He thinks he's so smart."

Right then I could have smashed Nancy in the nose; but as I looked up, I saw her grandma peering through the living room window. Grandma Wiggs' ugly face was pressed hard against the glass.

Just as soon as Nancy said, "Let's not buy," Patty stopped dead in her tracks and started walking back toward my stand.

At this same moment Paul Ellis came by. Paul was kooky. We used to call to him, "Pauly wants a cracker," and then he would really chase us. If he caught us, he would hit, scratch, kick and go violent. He never ever caught me, but he did catch Wally once and he beat the dickens right out of him. The Nelsons were going to sue the Ellises over that episode, but I guess neither had the money for court costs. The Nelsons always threatened that Paul was going to have to be put away. One day it came to me that to be "put away" meant to be placed in a special school for insane people. At first I thought it meant to be hanged or put in the gas chamber or something like that.

I asked Paul if he wanted to buy some lemonade, and he just grinned and showed me a nickel. When I saw that nickel in his hand, I got very excited. I quickly poured him out a glassful, and sure enough that nosey Nancy was right there to witness the whole transaction. I knew that Paul couldn't read. I could easily sell him one glass for his nickel, and he would never know the difference.

But that idiot Nancy just kept watching the whole business deal. Then I thought, "Now I've sinned because I wanted to cheat Paul." Then I made a short promise, "Lord, I really wouldn't have done that even if Nancy hadn't been there." I was getting in deeper and deeper with my lying and cheating and tried to push all of it out of my mind as fast as I could.

By this time Paul had drunk his first glass, and I poured him a second one but not quite as full as the first. Nancy didn't notice. Paul quickly gulped down his second glass. I then poured him a little less than half in his third glass which I felt was his five cents worth.

By this time Patty came over with her two cents and requested a glassful. I was happy. Nancy looked awfully upset and headed right for her house.

I poured Patty a glassful and she began drinking it. I looked into my container and there was only about a glass and a half left. I quickly poured myself three-fourths of a glass and drank it so fast that it burned my throat. By this time Nancy came running out with her money in her hand. I knew

63

I had won our little battle and felt extremely confident and pleased.

She placed her two cents on the table and said, "I'll take a glass of lemonade."

I said, "Okay, Nancy." I began to pour it from the glass from which I had drunk.

She asked, "Who drank from that glass?"

I said, "I did."

She said she wouldn't drink from my glass. This really made me mad.

I said, "You know what, Nancy? My stand is closed."

I was afraid she would take me up on the closing and take her money back.

She said, "Can't I drink out of that clean glass? I certainly don't want to get your germs."

I said, "How about Paul's?"

"Ick," she said.

I suggested Patty's. She said, "Fine."

I poured the lemonade out of my glass so that the lemonade passed right over the part where my mouth had been. I poured her lemonade right into Paul's glass.

She argued about getting only three-fourths of a glass of lemonade for two cents, and I just smiled to myself as I began to close up my stand.

When I put everything away, I counted my money. "Nine cents, not a bad day after all," I whispered to myself as I folded up the card table.

I quickly put everything back in the house and decided it was time to treat Billy-Boy nice for a change. As I started off toward Nymore to the candy stand, Nancy and Patty were across the street jumping rope. They jumped rope by the hours. They would tie one end of the rope to the telephone pole and that way one could turn and the other could jump.

I waited until I got about fifty feet down the street and then yelled, "Hey, Nancy!"

She stopped jumping and said, "Yes, what do you want?"

I said, "You know that glass of lemonade?"

She said, "Yes, what about it?"

I said, "You drank from Paul's glass and you're going to get kooky, Nancy. You're going to get insane, Nancy, and I hope you do!"

She immediately started crying and began chasing me down the block. I just opened up my motors and left her in the dust. I zigzagged down the sidewalk with all of my money jingling in my pocket. I headed straight for the Nymore Candy Store.

CHAPTER 10
Back to St. Philips

Finally my Cloverine Salve order arrived. It came in a cardboard tube. There were twelve cans of salve in the tube, not ten, and inside were twelve beautiful colored pictures. The instructions suggested that each can of salve sold to a customer entitled him to choose a picture. The pictures were of a mother dog and her puppies, Jesus praying, a grown-up cat, different seasonal scenes, a beautiful mountain, a bowl of fruit and a little girl.

I opened a can of salve and it was the most creamy looking stuff; it really looked peaceful in the can, not a blemish was on it, just smooth and rich looking.

The prize list was also in the tube. It was rolled up with the pictures. I looked the prize list over quickly but could not find the picture of the red bike anywhere. I couldn't believe it, but it was not on the list. I took the list to my mother. She said that they probably took the bike off the list, as it would take years to sell that much salve and earn that expensive of a bonus.

I was very downhearted until I saw the beautiful Boy Scout knife at the bottom of the page. It was black with two blades, a corkscrew and it even had a bottle opener. I quickly checked on the number of cans of salve it would take to get the knife; and much to my surprise, it only required twelve cans. The disappointment of the bike being removed from the prize list quickly left me, and the Boy Scout knife became a satisfactory substitute.

It took me the rest of that summer to sell the twelve cans of salve; and more than once, I was happy that I hadn't ordered a thousand of them.

Finally, a week before school was to start I sold my last two cans to Joe MacMillan. He said he would use the salve on his horses when they developed sores. I wasn't particularly interested in how he was going to use the salve but was happy to get the fifty cents. Joe didn't want the pictures. I couldn't blame him for that, as all that were left were a picture of some fruit in a bowl and another one of a little girl sitting in a rocking chair.

I sent my order off for the Boy Scout knife and decided that it would probably be a long time before I sold salve again.

Although I didn't mention it to anyone, I was really quite happy that the summer was coming to an end.

The stores downtown were full of back-to-school clothes. That was about all that the people were talking about.

Being Catholics, we went to St. Philip's School. Everyone else in Mill Park, including Wally, went to the Nymore Elementary School. I didn't mind the fact that Nancy and Patty both went there, but always wished that Wally and Joyce Edwards went to St. Philip's with my sisters and me.

The first morning was always the worst. We Catholics and the rest of the kids on the hill all walked down to the new highway to catch our buses. There were the usual sayings, "Here come those Kirtland Catlickers" or "There's that little two-fingered Catlicker" by the older high school boys. I sure hated them for what they said.

We would all stand on the highway waiting for our buses. The public school kids rode in a beautiful, yellow stub-nosed school bus. It was about the nicest bus in the world. It had fancy leather seats and the door opened in sections. When the bus stopped, the air brakes would blow air out in a "swoosh" sound that was most impressive.

Our old bus was made of plywood and was painted black with orange letters that read, "St. Philip's School." It was so ugly. It looked like an old black box coming down the road. You could never depend on it being on time. We used to stand there sometimes waiting for what seemed like hours until someone would come by in a car to pick us up and tell us that the bus had broken down.

The public school kids called our bus the Old Black Mariha; and, boy, would they laugh when occasionally it would come early. My sisters and I would get on and then the motor would usually stall. Our woman driver would try to start it and it would wheeze and groan. Finally it would get going. Then she would let the clutch out too fast and it would jump, lurching back and forth for the first twenty to thirty feet until we would pick up some speed.

If the public school kids were watching us, as soon as I got in I would run to the back and pretend that I was looking for something I had dropped on the floor. I would hide so they wouldn't see me. I wouldn't get up and sit down until I knew we were well out of sight.

Before I knew it we were on our way to school again. I had almost forgotten that fourth grade meant that all the boys would begin their training for becoming altar boys. This was always the big moment in the life of every St. Philips' boy, and for me it was no exception.

I wanted to be an altar boy in the worst way. I felt a little guilty that my desire was for the wrong reasons. I never felt any kind of special calling like Sister Louise said one would get when one was considering the religious life. I saw becoming an altar boy as my opportunity to be the center of attraction; and best of all, it would surely be the end for me to have to sit in the front of the church with all the other students.

On Sundays, as each family entered the church, the children were expected to leave their parents and go way up to the front pews and attend mass as one big student body. At low masses we recited in unison the Latin prayers and at high masses we sang.

I don't know exactly what got into me, but one Sunday I decided that I was going to sit in the back of the church with my mother. As we walked to church, we discussed my request. My mother kept telling me that I was going to get myself into trouble with Sister Louise. She pleaded with me to go to the front with the rest of the kids. I insisted that I was going to sit with her. Finally, as we approached the church entrance, much to my surprise, my mother gave in.

We walked down the center aisle and took a pew about, midway. My mother whispered while she nudged me in the ribs, "Better go down front, Billy, with your classmates." I pretended to be deep in prayer and avoided her words. After saying my opening prayers, I sat back in my seat feeling good about sitting in the adult section. It felt great to put my arm on the oak armrest that separated the pew from the main aisle. I had a clear view as I gazed down toward the altar.

My friends were beginning to arrive and they were slowly filling up the front rows. Just as the sanctuary light came on, several of my classmates went by my mom and me. They turned around and gawked at me as if to ask, "Billy, what are you doing there?" I pretended not to see them and again ignored my mother's second nudge. By now most of the congregation was seated and I knew mass would soon begin.

It was customary just before mass started for the sisters to make their entrance two by two. It was always a beautiful sight; the organist was playing a soft hymn, the main lights in the church were turned on and the sun would be shining through the stained glass windows. The sisters very reverently entered the church with their hands in prayer-like position. The sisters' entrance topped things off. Finally the main server would ring the bell, and the entire congregation would stand to greet the priest.

Just when the two servers came out to light the candles, I became panicky. I suddenly realized that Sister Louise would likely be coming down my side of the aisle. "Surely she will spot me sitting beside my mother," I thought. I decided I'd better let my mom have the aisle seat. I jumped up with the intent to change places; and at that very instant, as I left my seat, I felt a cold hand slip behind my head and onto my ear. In one continuous motion I left my pew and found myself walking side by side with Sister Louise. Sister Anne was on my left and somehow I was in the middle. It all happened so fast that in just a few seconds all three of us genuflected in unison, and I found myself sitting by Tom McAllen and Sister Louise.

70

After mass, as I came out of the church, I saw my mom waiting for me. She had the biggest grin on her face. I had planned to be angry and wear my pouty face, but one look at my mother made me realize that the whole scene must have been pretty funny. I could not keep from laughing with my mom. We couldn't even talk for a few seconds. She said it was so comical to see me go down the aisle. "Aren't you glad now that you and Sister Louise changed your mind? And the way you all genuflected together, it looked like you had practiced many times. I could hear your sweet voice during the entire service, honey," my mother said in her teasing sort of way.

On the way home, I told my mother that I was going to work hard to be an altar boy so that I could say goodbye to sitting in those front seats and kneeling on the hard kneelers.

Sister Anne was the nun in charge of the altar boys, and on the fifth week of school we were all called down to her room. She was the first grade teacher and she had a very large room which gave us ample opportunity to practice before we rehearsed in the church. Her room had a miniature altar raised onto a two-step platform for altar boy practice.

That was something when all of us fourth grade boys went down to Sister Anne's room. She talked to us about our responsibilities and then presented us the prayer card. The prayers that the priest said were all printed in black. She told us that we could not begin any practice sessions without first knowing our Latin prayers. After this announcement, we all went through the prayers with her in order to get the correct pronunciations.

There were certain prayers that I really liked. They were "The Confiteor" and "The Suscipiat." I got so I could say them really fast and with good emphasis. Even Wally and all of my other Protestant friends were impressed, and they often asked me to talk in Latin when we were just sitting around doing nothing. I felt very good about the fact that I could speak in two languages.

At first it was a threat to me when my Protestant friends would ask me what the Latin meant in English. I didn't know myself, so I learned that the best way to react was to say that it was pretty secretive; and that if they wanted to be a Catholic, then they, too, would be able to know the translation.

In the month of October, Sister Anne announced through Sister Louise in fourth grade that if anyone was ready for his prayer test, he could go down and see Sister Anne at noon. I knew I was ready even before the announcement was made because I had been practicing and really wanted badly to get on the altar.

The very morning the announcement was made, I decided that at noon I would go down to see Sister Anne. After we were told it was lunchtime and we went to get our dinner pails and returned to our desks, I began to get panicky, so I practiced by myself reciting each prayer. When I placed my syrup pail on my desk and began to take the lid off my pail, Sister Louise said, "William, you may say Grace." I was so dumbfounded that I couldn't for the life of me begin. Sister said, "Young man, how are you ever going to be an altar boy when you can't remember how to say Grace?" I turned beet red and began to get all hot and prickly. After some time I started to say, "Bless us, O Lord, and these thy gifts," but she interrupted and proceeded to call on George Cole who immediately knew what he was doing and recited the prayer without difficulty.

I ate my peanut butter sandwiches quietly. I took my good sweet time, for I knew that if I were to go to the playground I would get the teasing of my life.

When I left the room, I went immediately down-stairs toward Sister Anne's room while the rest of the class was outside playing. As I walked down the dark hall toward Sister's room, I practiced my prayers. I felt I was ready.

I knocked on Sister's door and heard her say softly, "Come in."

I said, "I have come to recite my prayers, Sister."

She smiled and said, "All right, William, do you think you are ready?"

She recited the prayers that the priest would say and then I was to say my part. We went through every prayer from "In Nomine Patre et Fillie et Spiritu Sanctus" to the "Deo Gratias." I was perfect and I knew it! She smiled and said, "William, you were very good, and do you realize that you are the first fourth grader to pass your test?"

I was elated but merely said, "Thank you, Sister; I have been really practicing, Sister!"

"I can tell," she said, and with that she placed a Holy Card in my hand. It had a picture of Jesus on the front side and on the back side it said some things about Jesus' Agony in the Garden.

I said, "Thank you, Sister. When will we be practicing on the altar, Sister?"

She said, "We have a group of fifth graders who were not ready last year but will be starting some time this week. You don't mind going with the fifth graders, do you?"

"Oh no, Sister," I replied, "that would be just fine, Sister!"

"All right, then, I will let Sister Louise know that you have passed and she will notify you when we will have our first practice."

"Thank you, Sister," I said. "Good afternoon, Sister," I said as I backed toward the door, opened it and left the room.

My heart was bursting with joy as I hurried down the hall. I raced out onto the playground to announce my feat to everyone in the class. I was no longer concerned about not remembering how to say Grace at noon. All of my classmates were amazed hearing of my good fortune. I really laid it on them concerning the difficulty of the ordeal. I felt that toughening the interrogation from Sister Anne was in order, and I did just that for as long as they would listen.

The day finally came for practicing on the altar. I was especially happy because I was excused from social studies to go to the church.

The first thing we did was to try on our cassocks and surplices. It seemed as though Sister had hundreds of them and it was the joy of my life trying them on. I finally found one that fit me perfectly. Not only did it go on great, but it had a zipper down the front just like the one Father Taggert wore. Sister Anne showed us our lockers. Sammy Adams and my name were clearly printed on white tape. She had placed the tape on our locker and there was no doubt as to who owned it--William Kirtland. We were told to take our cassocks and surplices home and have them washed and ironed. I knew my mom would be very, very proud.

Sister Anne and our group, which consisted of ten of us, went to the sacristy. The priests kept their vestments there. I had never been in there before. Was I impressed! There were hundreds of candles and all kinds of fancy golden candleholders. There were many cruets and Father's vestments were hanging in full display. It was a spectacular sight!

From the sacristy we entered the altar. The lights in the church were turned off and just the sanctuary light was lit. It was beautiful! We all genuflected in front of the altar and then Sister began to whisper her directions to us.

She told us that at first we were going to start out as candle bearers for the Sunday High Masses. Sister said that it was a great responsibility, and that we must think of it as an important start, and that we should be very honored. I surely didn't have a question in my mind about that.

She told us the stages we would go through, and I listened intently.

"First you are a candle bearer, then we will evaluate you at Sunday Masses. When we feel you are ready and have done your job well, you will become a main server at weekday Low Masses. You will also be scheduled for Sunday evening devotions during that same time period," she said. "Then a good time later, but it will come sooner than you think, you will be selected to be the main server at Sunday High Mass. That will be when you are really good and especially desirous and worthy. When you get to high school, we will consider you for carrying the incense and also to be a cross bearer. However, those positions are surely down the line in your altar boy life."

I was swimming with excitement and my long-term goal was to carry the incense pot. "Boy, oh boy, some day when I carry that incense pot will I be proud," I thought to myself. Being selected for that part meant that you made three grand entries; walking around with your partner was quite a spectacle. In fact, there was one time during High Mass where you would come out on the bottom step of the altar, all of the people would stand and you would incense them! To me that would be even a greater thrill than incensing the priest or the altar.

We went through our candle bearer routine. I really didn't need the practice because I had sat in church many times watching and dreaming that I was up there.

I was ready; in fact, Sister Anne asked me to genuflect as an example to the rest. I was ever so reverent and smooth, as that, too, I had practiced many, many times at home. In fact, I had practiced the whole mass, even the priest's part, as I could sing like a lark. I often went around the house singing Dominus Vobiscum-Et Cum Spiritu Tuo and all of the other Latin prayers that the priest and choir sang at Sunday mass.

When we finished practicing, we went back to school with our garb under our arms. I had missed nearly the whole afternoon of school; and before I knew it, I was on the bus and headed for home. I ran from the bus and told my mom all the news. She started the washing machine and my altar boy outfit was sudsing up to my delight.

That night I said all sorts of prayers thanking the good Lord for this special day. I went to sleep and dreamed all sorts of bad things: scenes like falling off the altar, hitting the priest on the head with the incense pot, and not knowing any of my prayers. On and on the bad scenes went. Finally I woke up. I was nearly exhausted, but happy it was a bad dream.

That morning my mother had my cassock and surplice all ready on a hanger for me. I left for the bus and ran through the neighborhood. I wasn't running for the excitement to get to school as much as I was running so that none of the neighbors, especially Wally, would see what I had. He would probably ask a lot of stupid questions. He might even tease me!

When I arrived at school, I found on my desk a schedule for the month. I could hardly believe my eyes, for I was on for the first two Sundays as the candle bearer. Sammy Adams and I were slated along with George Coles' brother, Tommy Granger, Bill Barton, and two college boys that I didn't know. They were the incense bearers. All of my classmates gathered around to see the schedule and they seemed to be as happy as I was.

For the first time in my life a Sister singled me out in front of the class. She stated to everyone that I was an example of hard work, desire, and prayer. Sister Louise said she had visited with Sister Anne, and Sister Anne had informed her that I was going to be a fine, fine altar boy. Everyone in the class smiled their approval to me. And at Sister's command they gave me a big hand.

Sunday finally arrived; the Mass went perfectly. After Mass, Father Taggert gave each of us a dime. He took the money from the collection plate.

For the first time ever, my dad went to church. After Mass, he told me he was awfully proud. Knowing he was in church and watching me on the altar had to be one of the most rewarding days I had ever experienced. I had done a lot of praying that one day my dad would come to our church, and now it had finally happened.

Being an altar boy slowly began to be old hat to me, and it became so routine that I soon graduated to the main server at daily and Sunday Masses. Like Sister said, "It will happen before you know it," and it did.

Every Friday afternoon right after lunch, Sister Louise would announce that it was the time to examine our consciences. I liked this day very much because it was an easy day as far as schoolwork was concerned. However, in the end when we filed over to the church for our confessions, my attitude was quite different and I became scared and guilty. I was especially frightened to tell one sin that I had carried on my soul for a long, long time. What happened was that Ann Novak used to sit behind me in class, and all of us boys would drop our pencils in order to try to see her underwear. It became quite a game; and because everyone did it, I didn't feel quite so bad about doing it, too. However, I never knew how the others felt about the sin and whether or not they told it to the priest because it was also a sin to discuss confessions with one another.

When Sister Louise said, "Put your heads down on your desks," and then began reading the list of possibilities, I tried to make the appropriate tally marks in my head.

Have I honored my mother and father? (most of the time)

Did I miss Mass on Sunday? (never)

Did I eat meat on Friday? (never)

Did I think bad thoughts? (Yes, I tried to see Ann Novak's underwear)

Did I lie? How many times? (Yes, three or four perhaps)

Did I use the Lord's name in vain? How many times? (Yes, way too many times; seven, I guess)

The examining of the conscience time was in a way pleasant and relaxing; however, going to confession afterward was what I feared the most. Thoughts ran through my mind and I had made my decision that today was the day I was going to tell it all and be truly free from my sins.

As we approached the church, I knew I had the courage and I was determined to go through with it. I was first in line. That was good! That meant I would be able to move right down to Father Taggert's box and would not have to confess to Father Rawling.

I went down the aisle, genuflected, and entered the confessional. As usual it was dark and I was scared stiff. Father Taggert slid the little door to the left and I could see the outline of his face. He was positioned so that I could get a good look at his profile. His blond hair was clearly in evidence to me and his face looked especially kind.

I crossed myself, stating, "Bless me, Father, for I have sinned; it has been a week since my last confession. And since that time I have used the Lord's name in vain about seven times; and, Father," my voice trembled and I wasn't sure I could go through with it. "And then, Father, I have been thinking dirty thoughts." It came out so fast that I even surprised myself. I sunk down into the confessional and waited for the worst.

Father then said, "For your penance you should say one rosary and promise not to do this again."

I quickly replied, "Thank you, Father; I won't ever do that again." I completely forgot all about all of the lies I had told.

Father said, "Remember me in your prayers!"

I said, "I will, Father. I will!"

I came out of the confessional with what seemed like one hundred tons lifted off my body. I was so happy that I was rid of that bad, bad sin. I ran back to the school saying, "Thank you, Jesus. I love you, Jesus. Jesus, Mary, and Joseph, pray for me!"

CHAPTER 11
The Horse Killer

Lois and Pat had put away the thank you cards and were out in the kitchen talking to each other about their children. Occasionally Lois would shout from the living room to me. "How about the time I was blamed by Peter Johnsen for starting a fire in Little Woods and Dad took me to the woodshed only to learn later that I wasn't there?" We all had a good laugh.

"Yes, I remember his saying that made up for the times he should have licked you for the things he didn't know about." Then we all laughed again.

"Mom, do you remember the old oak tree in our front yard?" I asked. My mother was very much surprised about my remembrance of such an insignificant thing as the oak tree in our Mill Park front yard.

Every year in the fall we picked acorns and took them across town to the zoo. They were fed to the bears and other animals over the winter. We got a penny a pound for all the acorns we could bring. It was my feeling that there were hundreds of dollars up there in that beautiful oak tree. The oak tree represented my extra clothes money for school, and I was looking forward to some really fancy duds.

All night long I thought about all the clothes I would buy. I wanted a leather jacket in the worst way. I liked those real tight long-sleeved knitted shirts with different colored stripes going across the front, and corduroys were really the kind of pants I liked to buy. I just prayed all night that I wouldn't have to get a pair of bib overalls. Boy, how I hated them! Poor kids wore bib overalls.

The next day I picked a whole wagonload of acorns and poured them into several large sugar sacks. I had a total of six sacks of acorns that would easily go about one hundred pounds. I went into the house and made myself a quick sugar sandwich and was on my way to the zoo. I started out on a dead run with my wagonload of acorns behind me. I was so excited to go to the zoo anyway, as I never grew tired of looking at the animals. I especially liked to look at the beautiful peacocks.

There was a baboon that was almost human, and I just loved to tease him. I was hoping that none of the zookeepers would be around so that I could be really mean to him. He was mean, too. He would climb right up the fence; and I'm sure that if he could have gotten out, he would have bitten me good. One time when we were teasing him, he threw some rotten oranges at Wally and sprayed his shirt with rotten orange juice. Wally's shirt never was the same after that because of the acid in the orange.

As I slowed down to a walk, I kept thinking of all the good things that were going to happen to me at the zoo. I was slowly approaching the stockyards when I heard several men back in one of the corrals talking. They were dressed up pretty fancy to be workers, and they were bent down over a horse that was lying on the ground. It was the big white horse; I could see his rear end from the sidewalk.

As I turned to climb the fence to have a better look, I noticed the sheriff's car coming up the road from town with its flashers and siren going full blast. I jumped down quickly because I wanted to make sure I would see where the squad car was going; and if it wasn't going too far, I intended to follow it. We always followed the cops and firemen when they came up our way because we got a big thrill watching them at work. I especially liked to see them wrestle with drunken men or arrest people; yet, I was scared to death of them, especially the sheriff.

As I climbed down from the fence, the siren was blasting very loudly; and the dust was blowing from the speed of the car that suddenly stopped right by my wagon. Several men stepped out, looking stern and serious. I knew they couldn't be after me because I hadn't done a thing wrong that I could think of. I was really happy that the acorns I had in my wagon came right from the tree in our yard. There was no question in my mind that I was in the clear.

The sheriff came right up to me and asked, "How long have you been here, Son?"

I was frightened but said, "I just got here and I'm meaning no harm. I've been picking acorns and was on my way to the zoo to sell them."

He said, "That's okay. There's no problem with you, but I was wondering if you had seen a man looking suspicious around here by the stockyards?"

I said, "No sir, I haven't seen anyone except those two men inside the corral."

The sheriff said, "Well, you go on about your business then."

I said, "Yes, sir," and I immediately started up the sidewalk.

As I went thirty feet or so, I stole a glance behind me to see if the sheriff and his men were watching. I noticed they were climbing the fence and jumping down into the pen where the men and horse were.

I stopped dead in my tracks and pulled my wagon over by the grass. I then slid between the fence boards to see if I could find out what was so secretive. As I crawled along the fence, I could hear the huddled sheriff and men mumbling about the white horse on the ground. I got close enough so I could have almost touched the sheriff's foot. I could recognize that big foot of his anywhere. Then I could hear them discussing the whole situation.

The dressed-up man said, "Why anyone would want to do this is beyond me." The sheriff suggested that it was the work of a crazy maniac. By now my heart was beating rapidly.

As I leaned up on my seat, I could just manage a much better look; and not three feet from me was the poor white horse's head. It had blood all over it. Its tongue was hanging in the dirt and horse manure. Its eyes were open looking straight at me. It was the worst looking thing I had ever seen.

As I looked at the horse's head, I could see a big gash right under its neck. The horse's juggler was clean cut. I'll bet the cut was a good ten to twelve inches long.

I almost started throwing up at the whole sight! My fear came back to me when I remembered the sheriff saying, "You get along and mind your business."

Just then the sheriff said, "We've got ourselves a horse killer on our hands, Frank."

They discussed what they were going to do about it and how they were going to catch him. One of the deputies suggested taking fingerprints.

"My God," I thought to myself, "there isn't a square inch of that place that I haven't been around; and I've ridden that horse, touched the boards and everything in the corral."

Then another deputy said, "Let's go get the bloodhounds." At that suggestion, the whole bunch took off for town.

I climbed out of the corral and took my wagon on a dead run, looking back at every step for fear the horse killer was right behind me. As I walked through town, all I could think of was my good old friendly white horse with blood all over him and his eyes looking right at me. I tried to get the scene out of my mind but then started thinking about the trip home. I suddenly remembered that it might be getting dark by the time I was on my way back, and I began to get frightened thinking I had to go back by the stockyards again. "What would I do if I ran into that horse killer and he came after me?" I thought to myself.

By now I had reached the zoo.

"Well, that looks like sixty pounds," the zookeeper said as he peered over his glasses. "How would seventy cents be on this fine day?"

I couldn't believe it! That's the most I had ever brought up on one load; and although I didn't want to appear too happy for fear he might not take any more, I said, "Thank you. Will you be taking a lot more acorns this season, sir?"

He said, "Yup, all you can bring in. It's going to be a long winter."

"Our oak tree hadn't even started dropping anything like it's going to," I thought as I left the zoo. As I walked by the monkey cages, I tossed several acorns in to the monkeys. They were pleased to receive my little gifts.

Then I came to Bob, the baboon; he was the one that we all teased. I picked up a rock and was going to throw it at him. He looked so innocent and sad that I decided instead of throwing the rock I would toss him my last acorn. I threw the acorn at him and stood there watching him shell it; he chewed it down in seconds. I felt good about being nice to him and trudged slowly down the sidewalk toward home. My wagon was light to pull, I had seventy cents in my pocket, and I was very happy.

I didn't bother to stop in town as I was in a big hurry to get home and begin picking another wagonload of acorns. I knew that I had to make the money while I had the chance. As I walked across the bridge, I began to catch sight of the stockyards and then my happiness quickly left me. "Oh, no," I thought out loud, "I wonder what happened? I wonder if they caught that horse killer yet? What did they do with the dead white horse?"

As I neared the stockyards all was quiet. I decided not to look in but just quickly walk by. As usual it started to stink as badly as ever, and I could tell that I was about halfway past the spot. I couldn't help but glance and catch a view of where I thought the horses were. Sure enough, they were gone but I could see the blood all splattered around one of the hitching posts. Suddenly I heard a noise; as I looked to my left, back in the shadows of the corral I could see two big rubber boots with some blue pant legs tucked inside the boots. The boots and pant legs were covered with manure.

I was walking so that if I were to go on for another twenty feet, I would be directly in the person's view, so I stopped dead in my tracks. I didn't know what to do. I was scared stiff. I was sure that the horse killer was back to find some more horses and maybe even people! I started backing up with my wagon handle in my hand when I saw the boots move forward a little, too.

I don't know what made me do it, but I lowered my voice like my dad's. I was pretty good at impersonating him, and I hollered as loud and as low as I could. "Hey, you, mister, what are you doing in there?" Then I turned my wagon upside down and pulled it back and forth on the concrete sidewalk. It made a big racket. At the same time I began barking like Shorty Oftedahl's police dog. I barked and pulled my wagon on the sidewalk. I shouted, "Sic um, Buck; sic um, Buck" and continued barking. All this time my eyes never left those boots. During the middle of my barking, scraping and hollering, the boots moved. About ten seconds later a man fully dressed in overall pants and jacket cleared the corral and was running down the railroad tracks. I righted my wagon and ran down the sidewalk in his direction. As I got by the stockyards, I could see that the man, too, was scared to death; and I watched his overall jacket wave in the wind as he continued to run down the tracks that bordered our neighborhood, Mill Park. Fortunately, he didn't go up the hill toward Mill Park.

I didn't seem to be nearly as nervous and afraid as I thought I might; in fact, I felt pretty proud that a grown man was afraid of me and that I had scared him off. I forgot all about the fact that he might be the horse killer until I crossed the tracks and looked down in the sand and could see his perfect footprints.

There was no question in my mind but that these were his tracks and that they were also the prints of the killer of the white horse in the stockyards.

I began to get nervous and weak, so I started to run for our house as fast as I could. My wagon had never experienced this kind of speed. I ran until I reached Bergstrom's house, always looking behind me and to my side for anything and anybody strange or foreign.

I felt pretty safe as I pulled my wagon under our oak tree. I ran into the house as fast as I could to tell my mother everything that had happened.

When I hollered for my mother, there was no answer. I yelled, "Ma", at least five times while I walked about the house but still no answer. "You don't suppose he killed my mother," I thought, when I happened to glance at the kitchen table and spied a note that was written by my mom: `Billy, when you get home be sure to fill your wood box. I am down at Malleys and will be home before Dad comes home for supper.'"

I felt better. My mom was okay and I was sure that the horse killer hadn't left the railroad tracks to come up to our neighborhood. "Why would he want to do that anyway?" I asked myself.

I walked out of the house and proceeded toward the woodshed. I was about to enter the woodshed when my eyes focused on our rhubarb patch in the garden. I decided to get myself a nice fresh stalk of rhubarb, as a little lunch before carrying in the wood would taste good.

I walked through the garden and reached the rhubarb patch and began spreading the broad leaves around in order to find a nice, tender red shoot. I turned and looked at the rows of corn, and something attracted my attention that caused me to walk over there. I saw an imprint in the sand. As I approached the disturbance in the dirt, I saw a set of tracks. "No, it couldn't be," I said aloud. But there in the sand was one footprint right after another. There was no question about it. They were his! And they were leading out of our garden right toward our house.

I was petrified; I couldn't move. My eyes must have been as big as saucers. The hair on the back of my neck gave me an eerie feeling. I stood there in the garden shaking like a leaf. Could he be in our house? Maybe he was in the basement! "Maybe he's in the woodshed!" I gasped.

Just then my dad drove into the yard. I was never so happy to see him in all of my life. I ran as fast as I could toward the car; and before he opened the door, I was there to meet him.

My dad asked, "What in the heck is the matter with you? What has happened? Are you all right?"

I tried to talk and nothing would come out. I couldn't even make a whisper come. Finally, I came to my senses. By this time my dad was frantic. He ran to the house and hollered for my mother. When I entered the house, I saw him reading my mother's note. He looked at me with madness in his eyes and said, "What in the name of God is wrong with you?" and he began shaking me. "Talk, for crying out loud, talk!"

Finally I was able to tell him the story, beginning with the scene by the stockyards, the killing and all. Then onto the zoo, then back to the stockyards. I said, "Then I changed my voice, 'Hey, you, what you doing in there? You'd better get out of there mighty fast.' It was something like that." I described the exact boot print to my father, and then I took him to the garden and showed him the boot prints.

My dad made a print of his own in the sand. I assumed he was checking to see if they were his. They weren't even anywhere near alike nor the same size.

We tracked the footprints toward the house. As the killer left the garden, his prints began to fade out on our lawn, so it was anybody's guess as to where he went after leaving our garden. He might have gone right straight across our front yard for the lake or the Great Northern tracks.

My dad started toward the woodshed and I was right behind him. I felt pretty darned proud and brave at this point. My dad said, "Who's in here?" His voice ricocheted and fell into the stillness of the wood and chips.

As my dad turned toward the house, I repeated his phrase, "Who's in here?" and received no reply. We were tough detectives, and I was now enjoying every bit of it.

We went into the house, opening up the closets and looking under the beds. There was nothing.

Then we started toward the basement. My dad said, "You better wait upstairs." I was glad he said that, as I didn't want to go down into that dark cellar. Then he said, "No, you'd better come with me."

I questioned, "Dad, don't you think we'd better call the sheriff instead of going down there?"

My dad said, "That's a good idea," and he came back up the steps. My dad shut the basement door and locked it with the skeleton key that was always in the door. I had never before seen him turn it to a locked position.

My dad went into the living room and took the phone in his hand. He was actually shaking while he told the operator that this was an emergency and that he wanted the sheriff's office immediately. At first he had a hard time spitting it out and I could tell that his voice was trembling. I knew now that this was serious business. In the meantime, I placed my ear on the middle of the heat register to listen for any possible strange noises that might be coming from the basement. There was no sound that I could hear.

My dad explained that the sheriff would be out shortly and that I was to stay out of his way. However, he said, "You tell the whole story to the sheriff. You can quit talking at the point when I drove up in the yard; then I will take over. In the meantime, we'll stay right here." I was really proud. Here I was right in the middle of a real crime, and my father was treating me like an adult.

We waited for what seemed like an eternity; never once did we hear a sound from the basement. Finally the sheriff was headed up Mill Park Road. We could hear the sirens blaring. "This would have to be one of the biggest things that hit Mill Park in a long time," I thought.

We went outside only to see the sheriff's car drive by our house with his sirens blasting and his lights flashing.

"That dumbbell," my father muttered, "he can't even read an address right." I felt he must be pretty excited but not dumb. How could he be a sheriff and be dumb?

My dad said, "I'll stay by the house. You run and catch them and show them to our house, Bill."

"Bill, Bill, Bill," I thought. How good that sounds when my dad calls me Bill. That means I'm big, I'm important, and I know my dad thinks I'm bigger now and I'm more like him. How good that sounded, "Bring them to our house, Bill!"

I ran across the front yard and trailed the sheriff's car down toward the dead end turn-around. I ran with my knees high and my toes kicking sand behind me. I was faster than ever and I was so proud because I was about the most important person on the block.

By the time I was past Oftedahl's, the sheriff was on his way back. The sirens were still screaming, the lights were still flashing, and I hoped he would never shut them off. I stood right in the middle of the road, crossing my arms back and forth to get the sheriff to stop, just like the brakemen did on the railroad. As he stopped, I ran right up and jumped on the running board of the sheriff's car. I hit my knee on the siren when I jumped, but it didn't matter; nothing could hurt me now.

I said, "Sheriff, are you looking for my house?"

He asked, "Are you Henry Kirtland's kid?"

I said, "You betcha, Sheriff, and I'll show you right where that horse killer is!"

As soon as I said that, the sheriff started right out with my holding onto the door, standing on the running board of his black squad car. The siren was still blasting away. It was so loud that I couldn't hear a thing. In fact, I never dreamed that siren was so deafening when you were that close to it. As we rode, I looked over on the sidewalk. There were people galore; some I had never seen before. All of them were following the sheriff's car. I waved to the crowd as we went by. Several people waved back to us. Nancy Wiggs, in particular, waved and I could hardly wait to tell all of them the whole story, how brave I was, the whole thing; it would be great!

I leaned in the window and said, "Sheriff, it's the white house. The one with the blue roof, 169 Gemmell Avenue. That's our house."

The sheriff drove right up on the sidewalk, across the front lawn and didn't stop until he was almost right by my father. I wondered if my dad would give him heck, because no one ever drove up on our yard like that. I leaped from the running board and the sheriff and his men jumped out of the car. They had pistols in their hands and one even had a long shotgun; it was, in fact, a double-barreled shotgun.

By this time there was a crowd gathered, a big crowd right in front of our house. Two of the sheriff's men went right to the crowd hollering, "Get back, there's a horse killer in Kirtland's house. He's probably dangerous and we're going to flush him out."

My dad pointed the basement door out to the sheriff and his men who slowly began walking down our stairway. When they were almost downstairs, my dad started running for the side of the house. While he was running, I, too, remembered that we had a basement window. I ran right behind my dad. When we rounded the corner of the house, we could both see the horse killer coming out of our basement window. He was just getting to his feet when we caught sight of him.

He started running at a fast gait for the front of the house. He ran right toward the crowd that was gathered in our front yard. My dad and I were right on his heels. Although I could run faster than my dad, I decided to hold back some for safety reasons. Even though I knew that I could beat my dad in a foot race, I was surprised at his speed.

We were gaining on the horse killer with each stride. As he ran into the crowd, the people parted and made him a pathway. Just as he was crossing the sidewalk and was in the middle of the road, my dad jumped him. He hit him high and held onto his arms, riding on his back. I hit him low and grabbed his legs. We all three went down with a thud.

The sheriff's men were there in seconds and held him down while another man handcuffed him. I was afraid to look at him. My dad and I were both trembling like leaves. The horse killer kept his head down while the deputies pushed him into their squad car.

All of our neighbors were smiling and some were even clapping. My dad and I were really proud of ourselves.

The sheriff told my dad that he was going to recommend to the mayor that my dad and I receive a special citation for our bravery.

Just then my mother came walking into the yard from Malleys. She wanted to know what all the commotion was about. She said, "Billy, you haven't been in trouble again, have you?"

My dad said, "Heck, no, Margaret. This little man and I just captured a criminal. Come on in the house and we will tell you all about it, hey, Son?"

I could have kissed my dad when he said, "Hey, Son?"

My father told my mother that this guy had apparently been working for Joe Macmillan down at the stockyards some years ago and that Joe had caught him stealing some of his beef cattle. The guy had been sent up to prison and had been released and came back. Over a period of time he apparently killed some of Joe's horses in an attempt to get even with Joe.

I asked my dad if he would try to get even with us or with me if he got out again. My dad said, "No, he doesn't even know who we are or how we knew he was down in our basement."

The whole episode cured me on our basement. I didn't set foot in it for a long time. I don't know how I was able to avoid it, but I made deals with Lois and Pat and my mother, and even talked my dad into giving me other chores; but no way was I ever going to go down into that basement again.

I was glad I never saw the killer's face, as for a long time I dreamed about those boot prints. For a long time I got my wood from the woodshed when the sun was overhead. I never wanted to go to that woodshed at night; and before I ever entered the woodshed, I always began announcing my arrival by hollering as loud as I could, "Hey there, anybody in here?"

CHAPTER 12
Moving to Littlefork

Each afternoon when school was dismissed, we all marched out to the playground to a phonograph record called "Catholic Action." As we marched we sang. We went down the stairs four abreast. Sister Teresa always stationed herself on the first landing. She also set the record in place and cranked the Victrola music. When she wasn't cranking, she was clapping to the beat of the music and kept an eagle eye out for any misbehavior. I sang proudly and as loud as I could:

> **"On earth's battlefields**
> **Never an advantage we'll yield,**
> **'Tis onward we'll always sing.**
>
> **Heads lifted high,**
> **Catholic action our cry,**
> **and the cross our only sword."**

The bus made a north end trip first and then came back to pick up those of us who lived in the Mill Park-Nymore area. We had about a twenty-minute wait.

Sometimes we played on the playground, and other times we helped get in the cook stove wood at the Sisters' house. I always wanted to carry in the wood because Sister Anne, who cooked, usually was good for a big cookie or an apple.

This particular afternoon, however, I sneaked off the playground and went down to the Glass Block Drugstore that was only one block from our school. It was fun to look at all of the good things for sale in the drugstore. With Christmas coming, I wanted to do some serious looking so that I could make out my Christmas list.

While I was standing on the curb ready to cross the street, a band came marching up the avenue. There was a small group of soldiers marching behind the band and following the band came a number of men who were also marching to the beat of the drums.

Everyone stood at attention with their hands over their hearts as the parade and flag passed by. I couldn't figure out what the occasion was, especially in December. Finally I asked a man near me, "Why are they having a parade on this cold day?"

He said, "Because we are at war. Don't you know that?"

"No, I didn't know that," I said. I asked him who we were at war with.

He said, "The Japanese and the Germans."

I said, "Who are they?"

He said, "Kid, don't they teach you anything in your school?"

I didn't say anything more to him as I didn't want to appear dumb or give him the impression that I hadn't learned anything in school. Besides, I felt that I came from a really good school. We learned a lot; in fact, Father Taggert had said several times that we could be very proud of the education that we received at St. Philip's School.

By now I realized I had missed the bus. I walked home slowly, kicking hard clumps of ice all the way, wondering why we were at war and how soon we would win. I began to wonder where the war was. I wondered why the Germans would be fighting us. My Grandma Schmit was pure German. I wondered what she would think of this war. I just never read of the Japanese and Grandma Schmit said that the Germans were good people.

When I arrived home, my mother told me that we were moving to a new home. I asked her if it was because of the war. She said, "No, Dad has received a promotion, and we are going to Northern Minnesota where he is to be a section foreman. He's going to be the boss now." There was a definite twinkle in her eye.

My mother said that my dad had already gone up to our new place and that this weekend he would be back in Bemidji to help us move. She said that we had plenty of packing to do.

"How long is it until Christmas?" I asked my mom.

She said, "Fourteen more days. You won't miss much school because of Christmas vacation."

That night my dad came back from his new job. He was really happy. I overheard him telling my mother that Littlefork was really a pretty nice place and that we could make a good home there.

I listened to my father talk to my mother in bed. "You know, Margaret, we will be better off to get the heck out of Mill Park. It's no place to raise these kids. And you know, Margaret, we can have a cow and chickens, pigs, stuff like that. With the war coming on, there is talk of meat shortages and it's a better place to raise the kids. And then, and then, we will cut down on expenses because we will live in the section house. We can sell our Mill Park house and that will buy us some livestock and . . . and . . . ." I drifted off to sleep.

The next morning we started packing. We packed our stuff in bushel baskets and cardboard boxes and what suitcases we had. We packed all of our furniture. We had an awful lot of furniture. We had our kitchen table, three beds and our washstand. My dad and mother's dresser went, my daybed too, and all of our bedding, not to mention the ice box and our living room couch that we bought at Dewey's secondhand store. It was a big job!

That afternoon Shorty Oftedahl came over with his gravel truck and he and my dad took all of our belongings to a railroad car. "We have free freight," my dad said, "and how can you beat the fact that we don't have to pay for moving our furniture and belongings? And our section house means free rent, too."

94

After packing and loading the boxcar, we went across town to my Grandmother Schmit's and stayed in her trailer house. We had to get up early that morning and ride the passenger train up north. I could hardly wait until morning, and as a result couldn't get to sleep. Finally my grandma's alarm clock went off and the five of us walked to the depot.

It was really fun to ride on the train. We rode for three hours and finally the conductor said, "Littlefork, Littlefork."

We all had shopping bags to carry as we headed for the end of the train. I looked out the window at Littlefork and there was nothing to see. There were no people, no houses, no buildings; all I could see was a tiny red depot with the word, "Littlefork", on the side of it. The depot wasn't made of brick like the one in Bemidji. The depot was right next to a small road that disappeared into the snow and trees. Up on a little hill were several Standard Oil tanks with a shed. That was it!

I asked my dad if this was the town.

"Shut up," he said, "and get off the train."

There was a man dressed in overalls to meet us. His name was Byron Andrews. He was one of the men who was now working for my dad on the track gang. "Byron is one of my men," my dad said. I soon learned that whenever my dad talked about all the workers under him, it was "the men" or "my men."

Byron took the things from my hand and said hello to my mother, sisters, and me. We went into the depot for a few minutes. The depot was sick and gray-looking inside with a high ceiling, lighted by one little light bulb. In the middle of the room was a potbelly, black, coal stove. Frank Fairton, the depot agent, came out and met us. I could tell from the way my father laughed at his comments and reacted to him that Frank was more important than Byron.

We stood around for a few minutes before going up to our section house. It was located up the tracks. My dad pointed it out to my mother through the depot window. It appeared to be about a quarter of a mile away.

The day was just breaking and it was terribly windy. All I could see was snow--lots of it, blue air, and plenty of trees. It was a very dismal sight. There didn't seem to be a town, and it was obvious we were stuck in the middle of the woods. I could see that our house was surrounded by several small shacks. Every building including our house belonged to the railroad company. The exteriors were all painted barn red.

"Let's go up and see our house," my dad said. We all left the depot and started walking up the tracks. It was so cold that the moisture in my nose began to freeze; it was 39° below zero! We all had to walk backwards most of the way. The snow was deep and it began to go over my overshoes and into my stockings. This was one time I walked with my big red scarf over my nose and face. I began to get a closer view of our house and what I saw didn't make me feel any better. It was just a big box, uglier than sin. It was very, very tall and skinny. It stuck out like a sore thumb. There were several trees in the yard and a shack for a garage. There was no way that the whole business compared to what we had in Bemidji. I began to get sick to my stomach.

We entered the kitchen. It appeared to be a shed attached to the main part of the building. My dad called it a "lean to." The windows were all tiny, separated by small panes of glass. The kitchen was painted a dark gray, as were all the other rooms in the house. It was the same color as the depot. The floors were a dark stained brown.

I kept looking out the window for the town but there was none to see. I didn't dare ask my dad about that again. There wasn't a single light in sight. My stomach started to knot up and I began to get a weird feeling. I felt worse than I ever had before, worse than when I had shoved the boy's head through St. John's window.

I couldn't get over those terrible-looking gray walls and ceilings. The electricity wires ran on the outside of the walls, and the lights were just light bulbs hanging from cords with gold-colored pull strings.

At first I thought the depot had looked ugly and couldn't believe anything could be uglier, but our house surely was. There wasn't a piece of furniture in there, except for a small rectangular iron stove. The stove had a stovepipe that went nearly all the way across the room. It had pieces of wire holding it to the ceiling, thus preventing it from sagging; yet, there were dips here and there that made it look terrible. I couldn't understand why there was no furnace like we had in Bemidji, and learned that it was because there was no basement. That's the only thing that made me feel good. There wasn't any basement! At least there would be no place for a horse killer to hide!

As I browsed around the house, I noticed my dad's men were outside beginning to bring our furniture up to the house. They had nearly everything in the house in just a few minutes. I looked out the window and could see my sled, assorted pieces of building material, my mother's clothes rack, several storm windows, and our washing machine all scattered around in the snowy yard. Everything looked bleak and cold.

By this time one of the men brought in our gunnysack full of potatoes that we had bought for the winter. He dropped them into the center of the kitchen. I walked over to the sack of potatoes and sat down, as there was really no other place to go or nothing else to do. The tears started to run down my cheeks. The more I tried to hold the tears back the harder they came. I tried desperately to keep from crying, for I knew my dad would probably give me a licking for not accepting his new assignment.

Suddenly the freight train was moving back and forth on the tracks, which were not fifteen feet from our house. Every time it came by our house it would cause the building to vibrate, squeak, and shake. Our few pieces of furniture that were in the house seemed to jump up and down. I had never experienced this before and wondered how we would sleep at night with all of that racket.

My mother came over to me and lifted up my chin. She put her arms around me. She, too, had tears in her eyes.

The two of us began to sob aloud. Pat was bouncing a ball on the uneven kitchen floor, and Lois was sitting on one of our kitchen chairs with her head in her arms. She, too, was crying. This was, without question, the saddest day of our lives.

All of a sudden we heard two long train-whistle blasts coming from the direction of the depot. The sound nearly scared me to death. By the time the big freight train had reached our house, the engineer let go with two more blasts. The noise was deafening! The furniture and everything in the house started shaking again. My sisters and I ran for my mother for fear the whole house was going to cave in. The four of us clutched each other until the train went by. When it finally had passed, we turned toward the door and saw my father's face.

My father looked at all of us. He had so many clothes on that he looked as wide as he was tall. He said, "Now what's wrong with all of you?" No one said a thing. "For crying out loud, do you all want to go back to Bemidji? Is that what you want?"

My mother said, "Of course not, Henry. It's just that we feel a little blue, that's all."

I wanted to say, "Yes, we do! Yes, we do want to go back to Bemidji!" But I knew my mother's response was what my dad wanted to hear.

It was obvious to me that we were stuck in this God-forsaken place, and there was little that we could do about it except to bawl our heads off!

CHAPTER 13
Dinah

Christmas came quicker than any time in my life. I used to sit back and count the days, but this Christmas just happened. Our Christmas tree was so small my dad placed it on an end table.

All of my Christmas presents were a big disappointment. The expected socks and mittens Grandma knitted did not fit. My bad-hand mitten was way too large and the good hand was too small. I think Grandma Schmit got mixed up on which hand of mine was injured. The corduroy pants my parents gave me were way too big, and the St. Christopher's medal I always wanted gave me the prickly itch. I just couldn't wear it without breaking out with bumps all over my body.

After Christmas, Grandmother Schmit came up on the train from Bemidji; it was really good to see her. We played whist in the evening hours. My grandmother and I were partners against my mom and dad. Grandma and Dad drank their beer while my mom and I had orange pop. This was the first time my dad bought the refreshments. I must admit that it was cozy with the fire blazing away in the barrel stove and all the good treats to eat and drink.

Our house began to look better and I became more accustomed to it. My dad had the men come in on painting sprees, and we soon got rid of that terrible gray for yellows and whites which made things much brighter and more pleasant. My mom made curtains for the windows, and we were able to put down some linoleum rugs that, although were very cold on the feet, were sure prettier than the dark brown floors.

I did miss Bemidji, especially because it was a much larger town. The town of Littlefork had one small main street and not more than two hundred houses that were all located about a mile from our section house. At least Littlefork was bigger than the one depot and the Standard Oil buildings that I thought to be the town.

One of the worst things I started doing was wet the bed at night. I was terribly embarrassed about it. No matter how hard I tried to stop doing it, nothing worked. My mother and dad must have discussed the problem with our friends and relatives as suggestions and ideas were constantly pouring in.

My Grandma Schmit told my mother that I drank too many liquids and ate too many juicy foods too late at night. She advised my parents to cut me off the liquids right after I finished supper.

My Grandma Kirtland said when I had the mumps they must have gone down on me leaving my kidneys awfully weak. Her remedy was two cod liver oil pills a day. When I took those pills, I became sicker than a dog. For days I would belch that terrible awful taste from those pills. After pleading with my mother, I no longer was compelled to take the cod liver oil pills.

My mom, bless my mom, simply said she thought that I was going through a stage and that I would soon outgrow it. She said she thought it had something to do with our move from Bemidji to Littlefork.

Every night when I wet the bed, I would wake up, slip out of bed and try to find an old sweatshirt or something absorbent that I could put over the wet spot. I would try to be as quiet as possible so that I wouldn't wake my mother. The moment I stirred, however, I could hear my mother coming up the stairway. She would be wearing her gray flannel nightgown and her blue bedroom slippers. In her arms would be flannel sheets, a pair of pajamas and a dry mattress pad.

"Hi, honey," she would say, and together we would change my bed.

I would plead, "Mom, I can do this by myself; why don't you go back to bed."

She would whisper, "Naw, it's no trouble; besides, that's what mothers are for, to help their boys when they need help." She would then give me a warm kiss, and I would go back to bed.

In the morning I would run downstairs, dress, and get the copper boiler out of the back shed. I would put the boiler on our kitchen wood stove and begin filling it with water or snow. Once in awhile I found myself muttering and being cross about getting in the water. I would feel sorry for myself having to go outside to pump the water on those below zero mornings. I would completely forget about how hard it was for my mother to wash the bedding and then spend the day drying the sheets, blankets and pajamas on our wooden clothes rack. My mom dragged the rack in and out of the house all day long. It seemed as though we always had my bedding drying in front of the stove. My mother never ever once complained about the extra work because she knew that I was terribly embarrassed and ashamed.

Watching my mother come up the stairs night after night and make me a warm, fresh clean bed and knowing how difficult it was for her to wash and dry the sheets and blankets the next day caused me to love her more than ever.

I vowed to myself that some day I would write a long letter to the Bishop or the Pope and nominate my mother for Sainthood. I promised to myself that when I became an adult I would start the campaign. I would have written the letter right away, but I did not want any more people knowing that I was a no-good bed wetter.

Slowly, but surely, I quit wetting the bed. I was never so happy in my life. I never forgot how wonderful and understanding my mother was. Whenever the priest talked about the Sainted Mother of God, I always thought of my mother. I called her Sainted Margaret Mary. It had a beautiful ring to it!

It also took me a little while to get used to school. For the first time I was riding a bus like all the other kids. It was a much better bus than I had been used to. It was more like the public school bus the kids rode in Bemidji. My school was not nearly as nice as St. Philip's, but all of the kids were pretty friendly; and for quite a while, I was ahead in my studies in comparison to them. It took me a long time to quit calling the teacher, "Sister." I couldn't understand why all of the kids thought that my calling our teacher "Sister" was so funny.

Another thing that bothered me about Littlefork was when the county nurse came to our school. She helped our teacher with various health lessons. We studied about body cleanliness, dental care and the harmful effects of alcohol and tobacco. She would come in our classroom and give us what she called "oral quizzes." After nearly every classroom visit, she would ask to see me in private.

"Billy Kirtland, I would like to visit with you in the hall, please," she would chant in her singsong voice.

When I came into the hall, she would shut the classroom door and then proceed to examine my hand and stomach. While looking me over, she would ask the same old questions and write the same old answers on her same old charts. I used to get plenty tired of the whole ordeal.

My new Littlefork classmates were always very interested in knowing why she wanted to see me. I was afraid they would think that I had lice or had some disease that we were studying in health.

When I complained to my mom about the nurse, she said, "Oh, be a good boy and cooperate with her; it's only for your own good. Can't you see she is interested in you?"

What I soon discovered was that she was beginning to get me ready for a county side crippled children's clinic. The State of Minnesota was attempting to find out more about all of us crippled children and determine what they could do for us. With so much infantile paralysis going around, there seemed to be a lot more crippled children.

One Saturday, I boarded a Koochiching County school bus. All of us crippled kids headed south for Blackduck. There were two children from International Falls already on the bus when I got on. I was the only person from Littlefork. As we journeyed down the highway, we made stops for other kids at Big Falls, Mizpah and Northome. Our numbers increased to a total of seven in all. We sure looked out of place in our big thirty-six-passenger school bus.

I tried to talk to a boy from International Falls about what happened to him that caused him to limp. He wouldn't even answer me. A girl from Big Falls seemed to have problems raising her arms. When I asked her if she had gotten polio, she told me to mind my own affairs. No one wanted to talk to anyone. They seemed to be ashamed of their problems. I could have cried. It was so sad on that bus; immediately I became angry with the county nurse and my mother for getting me into this mess. Then I caught myself and thought about what my dad always said, "Billy, don't you ever be ashamed of your hand. Make the best of it. Never hide your hand or refuse to talk about it. People just want to know what happened. They are naturally curious."

I thought that if only these kids had a dad like mine, they wouldn't be so unhappy or afraid to discuss their problem.

Whenever I started feeling sorry for myself, my mom would say, "Billy, we all have some kind of a cross to bear." I spent the rest of the ride looking out the bus window just thinking about my parents' advice.

When we arrived in Blackduck, we went to the high school gymnasium. Other busloads of kids arrived from Beltrami, Lake of the Woods and Itasca Counties. Some of the kids seemed to be better and some worse off than me. Some of the kids were in wheelchairs and some needed crutches to help them walk.

We were all given a white gown and escorted to the locker rooms where we undressed and put them on. The gowns were of the hospital type having little strings in the back that the nurses tied for each of us. I hated having her help me with my gown and worse yet, having to parade around the gym wearing nothing but a gown. I couldn't understand why I had to get into that outfit just to have the doctor look at my arm and stomach.

There were various doctors stationed all over the gym. We were being examined by some high-powered specialists. The nurses guided us to each doctor. We had to lie on a little table while the doctor examined us. While I was lying on the table, different doctors came by and looked at my hand and stomach, then my hand, then my stomach, over and over again. Each doctor would say, "Hmmm", and then write some information on his chart.

A really tall, heavy-set doctor came to my table and started talking to me.

"So you are Billy," he said trying to warm up to me.

"That's right, Doctor," I replied.

"Well, Mr. Billy, what kinds of things can you do with your hand?" he asked.

"I can do lots of things," I responded.

"Such as?" he challenged.

"Well, I can pick up coins, tie my shoes, button my shirt, and arm wrestle," I said proudly.

"And what can't you do, young man?" he asked.

"There isn't much I can't do. Let's see, I can't climb a rope hand over hand, I can't do over fifteen really good pushups in a row, and I can't be the wheelbarrow in a wheelbarrow race, but I can hold the other guy's legs and wheel him," I said.

"Hmmm," he said and wrote on his chart.

I expected the doctor to say, "That's pretty good," or "Boy, you sure have done well with your handicap," but all he said was, "Hmmm".

Finally, after a number of doctors examined all of us, we went to the cafeteria and had a very nice lunch. We even had ice cream for dessert.

While eating lunch, I sat with a boy who was from Grand Rapids and who lost his right arm in a corn picker. He was the first crippled person that was willing to talk to me. I told him I wished he were riding back home on the bus with me.

After lunch was over, we went back to the gym for our consultations.

Two doctors and a nurse wanted to know what I thought of the idea of having a little surgery on my hand. They told me that they wanted to fix my wrist so that it would be more flexible. They also said they could straighten my hand out and clean it up so that it would look better.

I told them that I didn't mind the way my hand looked; and as far as I knew, it didn't bother my friends or my parents. I asked them if the operation would hurt a lot. "Some," the doctor said. "But you will be sleeping," he added. I asked them if I would be able to climb a rope after my operation. They said that it was doubtful that I would get any more use out of it but it would improve the looks of it. I asked them about football and other sports. "Will it help me be a better player?" I asked. They were surprised that I wanted to play football; they said that I should consider giving it up. When they could see that I became very disappointed, they said that they would be writing a nice long letter to my parents and that the Koochiching County nurse would help my parents make the decision.

As I rode home on the bus, I practiced the talk I was going to give my parents about this operation. It was going to be a very long-winded speech. By the time I was dropped off by the depot, my talk became short and simple: "Mom, Dad, I'm not going to have any operation on my hand, no matter what!"

Several weeks later the letter arrived. The county nurse met with my parents. My parents went over the same things that the doctors told me. We examined all of the facts and the decision was made. NO OPERATION!

Good things began to happen! I met a girl named Mae Robertson. She was in my class. I liked her right off the bat and she liked me, too; I could tell. She had short hair and bangs that were kind of square cut. She had the prettiest smile I ever saw. It was really a good feeling that I was special in her eyes. She used to get milk from the same farmer that we did. Getting the milk was one of my new jobs and I liked doing it.

I began to develop a routine. When I came home from school, I would make myself a peanut butter sandwich; and with my onion sack in hand, I would head over past the fairgrounds toward Garritys, who were the milk people. The Garritys were very friendly. Mr. Garrity was always happy to see all the people come for their milk. I used to love to hang around the farm. Sometimes I could clean the barn; and if I were lucky, Mr. Garrity would let me pitch hay down for the cows from the hayloft.

One night I was in the hayloft pitching hay to the cows when, to my surprise, Mae was coming up the ladder. I asked her what she was going to do in the loft and she said that Mr. Garrity said she could come up. For the longest time I pitched hay like a good trooper. In fact, Mr. Garrity hollered up and said, "Hey, Bill, that's way too much hay down here. What are you trying to do, feed the cows for a month?" When he said that, I discovered I was in some kind of a trance with Mae around; and I knew that I would do anything to impress her.

While I was climbing down the ladder, Mae came over to go down, too. When my head was about even with the hayloft floor, I looked up and just then Mae kissed me! Right on the lips, of all places! I was so startled I just gripped the ladder, not knowing what to do. Finally, when I came to my senses I climbed down the ladder. I ran out of the barn and to the milk house as fast as I could go. I grabbed my onion sack with the two full quarts of milk and took off for home. I was still running when I passed the fairgrounds. I stopped about a quarter of a mile from our house and then slowed my run to a walk. As I looked over my shoulder, I could see Mae crossing the bridge on her way home. I couldn't see the outline of her face but I knew it was Mae. She waved to me from the bridge. I looked around and there was no one else visible, so I waved back. I felt the warm kiss on my lips, the first one of my life. I slowly lumbered on home, whistling as I went. There was no question about it. I was madly in love with Mae!

It seemed like no time had elapsed before spring arrived. Everyone in school talked about the possibility of a long mud vacation, as there had been more snow during the winter than ever before.

Littlefork was primarily a farm and pulpwood community. Many of my classmates lived on small farms with their fathers earning part of their income from cutting pulpwood and the other part from the milk and cream their cows gave.

As expected, the roads were quick to go to pieces that spring; and, as a result, many of the farmers had to bring their milk and cream to town by either horse or tractor. When the frost left the roads, the bottom fell right out of them; thus, the buses could not pick up the kids for school. We finally had our mud vacation! I learned that school might be out for as long as six weeks. It seemed like a good thing to me and I looked forward to it.

On April Fool's Day, my dad told me that my mother would get the milk at Garritys and that he and I were going to go out in the country to pick up a cow that he had bought. At first I thought it was an April fool's joke but then remembered my dad discussing it when we lived in Bemidji. He also told me that he had ordered one hundred chickens from the Montgomery Ward's catalog and that he had me in mind to care for the "farm." He said that having a cow meant a lot of work but that he felt I was ready for the responsibility. "Along with the cow, we will have a pig, maybe even two pigs," he said. "And if you do your jobs, I think we can talk about a way to get you a calf to raise for your very own. This way you can have your own spending money from the profits you earn."

By this time my head was swimming. Was this an April fool's joke? I was so excited about the idea of having pigs, chickens, cows, and calves. Imagine us as farmers!

We ate quickly. While eating my dad winked at me. I was so taken up by it that I didn't know what to say or do. Finally I said, "Where is the cow now, Dad?" He said that we were going out to Williams' and that he had bought the cow for $97. She was already bred and hopefully would be a really good milker. He also said that she was dry now but when the calf was dropped it might be all mine. "Bred," "dry," and "dropped" were all terms I didn't know a thing about; and when I asked questions about them, I would only become more confused trying to understand my dad's new vocabulary. I could tell that my dad didn't want me to use those words in front of my mother so I dropped the questioning. I supposed it must have been man talk.

When we finished eating, we began walking into the country on the Linford Road. It was very muddy and I now began to realize why school was out for mud vacation. Alongside the road were patches of snow in the brush and woods. There were some pussy willows about ready to sprout. It was a colorless scene, but somehow one could just tell that things were going to soon look beautiful and that there were many wonderful, exciting things that were going to happen.

As we walked down the road, I kicked rocks and dirt clumps until my father told me to stop it because he didn't want me to wear out my boots. He reminded me that I had just used my last shoe stamp for this six-month period. We were just beginning to feel the war shortages of shoes, candy, gasoline, meat, sugar, coffee and things like that. During the entire walk to where we were going to get our cow, my father carried a beautiful black leather halter that one of the men had made which would soon go on our cow's head. Every once in a while I would run a little bit in order to keep up with my dad's gait.

Finally, after a long walk, we came to a little farm that was similar to Garrity's. They had Jersey cows on this farm, whereas Garritys had Guernsey cows. Jersey cows had black faces and noses. My dad told me that Jerseys didn't give as much milk, but their milk was richer; and as a result, we would have more cream. That seemed fine with me.

Don Williams, the owner of the farm, came out and said hello to my dad and he ruffled my hair.

He said, "Hank, is this your boy?"

And my dad said, "Yes, this is my son, Bill."

I wasn't sure of what to say so I said, "Boy, you sure have a really nice farm here, Don." Later my dad said I was to call him Mr. Williams, not Don. My dad could get that way, but who was I to argue.

Finally, after Don and my dad talked for a few minutes, we went to the barn to get our cow. The barn was dark and dreary, and it stunk to high heaven. Don obviously didn't take care of his barn like the Garritys did. The outside of the barn was all tarpapered with laths holding the black paper to the walls; and it, too, didn't compare to the nice red paint Garritys had on their barn.

We walked down through the barn and as we did, we saw lots of cows. The cows seemed to see us as intruders in their home and they scared me a little bit. I knew, though, that with their heads locked in the wooden stanchions they could not do us any harm.

Then we went by the bull. His head was twice as big as the cow's. He looked so mean. His eyes just glared at me. I managed to get right by Don and my dad for fear he might come after me. He started to move around, jockeying his rear end back and forth as if to try to get his head unlocked.

By this time I had forgotten why we were in the barn until Don said, "Well, Hank, there's your cow." I took my eyes off the bull for a split second to see our cow. She was lying down chewing her cud in such contentment. I couldn't see her face but I knew it must have been beautiful. Don kicked her in the rump and said, "Get up, boss." I was so mad at Don for kicking her that I could have kicked him for her. "She's having a hard time getting up, as she is soon to calf," Don said. He kicked her again, and this time I hoped she could get up quickly for fear he would do something meaner. She finally struggled to her feet; and when she did, she humped herself all up and went to the toilet right in front of us. Don suggested that maybe he "kicked the crap out of her" to which my dad and Don laughed. I was embarrassed, so I tried to act like I hadn't heard what Don said. I felt sorry for our cow and for me.

When I went around to try to see her face, I saw the other side of her body. She was all covered with old and fresh cow manure and then for sure I disliked Don Williams. I vowed then and there that this cow would have a much better home with us; I would see to that!

We backed her out of the stall and Don and my dad put her halter on. My dad gave me the chain to hold while he wrote Don his check. This was the first time I had seen my dad write a check, as we had never had checks before. I knew we were coming up in the world but didn't realize it was that fast, as the only people I knew who wrote checks were the Malleys in Bemidji, and they were plenty rich. I remembered that they had a new car and a nice home and always had a fruit bowl on their dining room table. Imagine, us writing checks! Maybe we would have a fruit bowl on our table soon!

My dad led our cow out of the barn and into the yard. Don wished my dad good luck and said good-by to me. He also suggested that I could come out to the farm any time I wanted to. I thanked him for inviting me; and under my breath said, "I wouldn't come back again to this farm for all the tea in China." That was an expression my dad often used, and I felt it to be a fitting one for this occasion.

When we started out and down the road, it began to sprinkle. We hadn't gone but about one hundred feet when it began to rain pretty hard. By the time we had gotten about halfway home, the rain was coming down in torrents. The manure was pretty well washed from our cow's hide, and she was beginning to look more and more beautiful. It wasn't long until we could see our red section house. All three of us were soaked to the skin.

When we got halfway between our house and the depot, I began to get excited about how my mother would react to our new cow. My sisters, too, would no doubt be waiting for our arrival. I was glad that it had rained, as she was nice and clean for our grand entrance into the yard. When we neared the house, our cow stopped dead in her tracks and began to bawl. "Moo-oo, moo-moo," she cried in a very mournful way. I wondered if she felt like I did when we moved. My dad pulled on the halter but she wouldn't budge. We tried everything but she refused to go up the hill and into our driveway.

I could see my mother and sisters' faces in the windows looking at us. My dad said, "Take her tail and start twisting it. That will make her go." When I began twisting her tail, she took off. I had a hold of her tail and my father, the chain. She started to kick all four feet and bucked like a horse with her feet flying in all directions. I hung onto her tail and my father, the chain. She went lickety-split across the front yard and around the house. She was bellowing like mad. My dad was cussing and hollering, "Whoa, whoa Boss, whoa!" She ran around the house two or three times, crazier than any animal I had ever seen. Between bellows and kicks, it was some scene.

When we finally had her settled down, my mom, Lois, and Pat came out and they were laughing like I had never seen them laugh before. My dad and I both had manure and mud all over us; and I looked at my father standing there with the chain in his hand, his glasses covered with mud and manure. White foam was dripping from our cow's mouth. The whole thing became very funny to me, too. We all laughed for quite a while. I got up on the cow's back and my mom snapped a picture of us.

We led her into our little barn; it was nice and clean and ready for her presence. She went in and seemed to be happy to be there. As we walked out of the barn, we saw a beautiful rainbow stretched across the horizon. While we walked to the house, I knew that we were going to talk about the whole episode.

The first thing we did was to discuss naming our cow. Everyone had a suggestion. My mother thought we should call her Dinah for dynamite that seemed to fit the way she acted. We voted on it and it was unanimous. Dinah was her name!

That night, throughout the discussions, I went to the little barn no less than five times to look at Dinah and talk to her. On the fifth visit she was lying down. I was happy that she was satisfied with her new home. I brushed her several times on the rump; and when I left the barn the last time that night, I looked up into the sky and thanked the good Lord for being so good to us. I just knew that our future was going to be filled with much happiness.

CHAPTER 14
Peaches - Peaches

I was really happy when my father told all of us that Don Williams had said that Dinah would be dropping her calf in May. In fact, the month of April was nearly half over, and that meant that in about fifteen long days we were going to have an addition to our farm family.

Our small farm was truly showing signs of spring. Our one hundred chickens arrived in the mail, and my dad was negotiating with Don Williams about purchasing a bull calf for the following year's meat.

Almost every other day Dad's men from the track would be up to build the various sheds that were to house the chickens, the pigs, and the calf Dinah was soon to drop. Dinah's calf and Don's bull calf would stay together, my dad suggested. The pig pen was completed and two little pigs that had been purchased from Kelley Pettis were placed in their new home.

It seemed like every night I came home from school something new was happening. I was very busy with all the chores. After my work, I would have time to change my clothes, eat supper and then listen to Henry Aldrich, Fibber McGee or Lux Theater. I was a very tired boy who went to bed, woke up early, did the chores, went to school, came home, did the chores, and then started the next day all over again. I seemed to be much more responsible now; and in order to make sure I didn't foul up on any of my duties, I made a schedule for myself. Every night I checked off each item so that I wouldn't miss any of them:

4:00 - Get off school bus and walk to house
4:30 - Get in wood and water
4:45 - Feed Dinah and clean barn
5:00 - Feed chicks and water them

114

5:15 - Feed pigs from buttermilk cans mixed with
       middling
5:30 - Check with Mom to see if she is going to wash
       clothes; if so, pump water for the boiler
5:45 - Go get milk at Garritys
6:15 - Supper
7:00 - Henry Aldrich or listen to other radio program
7:30 - Fibber McGee or listen to other radio program
8:00 - Spelling or any other school work
8:15 - In bed

I lived by my schedule and I was pretty proud of the fact that not once did my dad scold me for not doing my chores. One evening my dad asked me what I thought of the idea of receiving a fifty cents a week allowance. I couldn't believe it! Getting paid for my work! My dad said that I might be able to save a lot of money for my college education. The whole idea made me feel very happy. I continued to think about the matter that night when I went to bed. Boy, oh boy, inside of five months I would have ten dollars!

Then I started thinking that if my dad could buy a calf from Don Williams for $2, why couldn't I buy one, too, and then sell it later for a lot more money? "After all, he did mention it once," I reminded myself.

I talked with my dad about the idea the next night at the supper table. He had finished his supper and I knew he felt pretty good. I had declined to take my two wieners, even though I knew I was entitled to them. This left one extra for my father which I knew would make him happy. I had everything ready and was fully prepared to present my proposal to him. My hair was in place and well watered down for the occasion. After some discussion and all the promises made on my part, my father said he wouldn't let me buy a calf, but that he had an even better surprise. "How would you like to have Dinah's calf for your very own, Billy?" he asked.

Dinah's calf?! Not Dinah's calf?! Dinah's calf?! Those words ran through my mind. Could it be possible that my dad said he was giving me Dinah's calf? The tears ran down my cheeks; I looked at my dad with more appreciation than I had in my entire body. I put out my hand to shake his and said, "Dad, I'll take care of this farm like you would yourself."

I went to bed that night thinking of what that calf would look like when it came. How soon would it come? Would it be a bull or a heifer? It would definitely be a beautiful calf, that's for sure. But where would I get a halter? I'd make one, of course. Imagine! My very own calf!

In the morning I dressed quickly to go out to our little barn to see Dinah. "Maybe she'd dropped our calf," I thought as I went to the barn. When I opened the door, Dinah was lying down. I looked everywhere in the barn, but no calf. I was very upset, but then I saw that the gutter was full of manure and was happy that my calf hadn't come to fall in that mess. I quickly cleaned the barn and put lots of straw in the gutter in case my calf came while I was at school.

Every day when I came home from school, I ran straight from the bus, went directly to the barn or to our little pasture that surrounded the barn, and attempted to find Dinah, but every day there was no calf. I began to give up hope; however, watching Dinah get fatter and fatter told me that there was a baby calf inside her and it was going to be mine.

The school days were coming to an end, too slowly to suit me. Tests were hard, especially because I hadn't studied much. I was just marking time. Friday was to be the last school day, and I was especially looking forward to the summer vacation. We all lined up for our report cards and everyone was concerned about being promoted or being retained.

When Mrs. Jacksteadt handed me my card, I turned it over for a quick glance; and sure enough, it said, "William Kirtland is promoted to grade seven." Underneath the signature was a space for comments where she had written, "He could do much better if he worked harder."

When the bus let me off at the depot, I was one happy boy. Even though I was pretty well loaded down with my notebooks and odds and ends from my desk, I found it easy to run down the rails heading for our house.

As I approached the yard, my report card fell to the ground and I picked it up with, "He could do much better if he worked harder", staring me in the face. "If only she hadn't written that, it would be a perfect day," I thought. Visions of my dad chewing me out came into my mind and then the day didn't seem to be so nice. "There's always something like that which spoils things," I thought as I trudged into the yard. As usual, I surveyed the yard and the tarpaper sheds that surrounded our house. The grass was just beginning to turn a little green, and there were some buds on the popple trees.

My eyes moved over the fenced pasture area for Dinah. I caught a glimpse of a very tiny, brown figure just beyond a clump of brush by our little barn. "My gosh," I said to myself, "there's a little deer in our pasture." It wasn't really uncommon for the deer to come that close to our house. Yes, this was a baby deer!

I slowly eased my belongings to the ground and began crawling on my hands and knees until I was behind our very huge woodpile. The long ranks of wood were waiting to be chewed up by our saw rig. I knew I was out of view of the little deer. I slowly crept up the side of the woodpile, and my intention was to pop my head up quickly to get a good view of the little fawn before she would scamper into the woods.

I was ready now, as high as I could get. I lurched upward to scan the pasture and get my quick look. When I sprang upward, I could see the whole pasture, the barn, pigpen, chicken yard--a total panoramic view of the back yard.

Much to my surprise the deer had gone. I did spot Dinah feeding on the grass shoots, but no deer. As I began to climb down from my vantage point, I noticed a brown figure just behind Dinah; and it seemed to be butting her in the hind flanks. I could see some little legs just behind Dinah's big body. It didn't run away, but instead, it was hiding right behind our cow. I sat there observing it for several minutes. As Dinah moved ahead for more grass, the deer moved with her. I could tell it wouldn't be but a few minutes and I would get a good look at the little fawn as Dinah moved forward cropping grass.

Dinah spotted a bunch of clover and took about five steps forward. I knew I was going to get my look that I had patiently waited for. Finally, the little deer came into view. It was brown with a white patch on its forehead, and it was as cute as it could be. I must have looked at it for about three or four minutes; then I noticed its tail. It was brown and long, not short and white.

I began to wonder why that was. This wasn't a deer. "Holy smokes," I gasped, "that's Dinah's calf! Dinah's calf came today. That's my calf!" and down the woodpile I went as fast as my legs could carry me. I went straight for my calf.

At this very moment Dinah spotted me and made the strangest reaction. She headed straight for me with her head down. I couldn't believe it; all the nice things I had done for her and she was attacking me! I ran quickly behind the electric fence and began to talk to her. She just hummed and stared at me.

In the meantime, my calf let out a blat and kicked its heels, running around in circles like a little goat. It was still partially wet, and I immediately came to the conclusion that it hadn't come into the world but a few minutes ago. Maybe it was when Mrs. Jacksteadt gave me my report card, or just when I got off the bus; but that didn't matter. The calf was here and it was mine!

What really did matter was that I couldn't hug it and brush it and check to see if it was a bull or a heifer. Darn that Dinah! Why was she so protective? I quickly said a short prayer. "Jesus, please make it be a heifer." Then I thought, "How selfish, it's here, what difference does it make?" Then I prayed again. "Thanks, Lord, for bringing me my calf on this wonderful, wonderful day."

I quickly pulled some sweet grass from my side of the fence and walked slowly toward Dinah. I knew she would like that; and, sure enough, that was more important to her than our calf. I approached her cautiously; and while she was attending to the grass, I put my arms around my new friend. "You peach," I said to myself, "you're mine, all mine, you little basket of peaches! Oh, peaches, you're some kind of a deer." As I put my hands around its body, I slipped my hand between its legs to find out what I really owned. As I felt around, I found nothing; then I felt four tiny, soft, little knobs on her skin. "I've got myself a heifer! I have a heifer calf and pretty soon she will be a cow, and she's all mine!" I whispered to myself.

I ran for the house as fast as I could to announce our new addition to my mother. We both came out and looked at her. My mother's face was as happy as mine. Pat and Lois came out and they stood behind the fence as I pointed my calf's head toward them.

"What's the calf's name?" Lois asked.

My mother chimed in, "What are you going to name it, Billy?"

Geez, I hadn't thought about it; of course it needed a name, a special name. "PEACHES!" I said with no hesitation. "I'm naming her Peaches."

That night I went to bed the happiest boy in the world. I could hardly wait for morning. There was no school. I would have to begin making Peaches a halter, and I needed a special brush for Peaches. There were lots of things to do. "My gosh," I thought to myself as I lay in bed, "Dinah might lie down on her and kill her! Would she?" I called downstairs to my dad, and he assured me she would never do that. "Yup, she's my Peaches," I said to myself. I pulled my big comforter over my head and smiled myself to sleep.

CHAPTER 15
Summer at Last

Littlefork was slowly beginning to be a better place to live, and I was feeling more positive about it each day. My dad was more at peace with himself; and, as a result, I wasn't getting the lickings that I used to get in Bemidji. We seemed to be getting more new things for the house each month. When the Gambles' Store men moved our new Coronado refrigerator into our house, I was perhaps the proudest person in the area. It meant two things: no more ice water to take care of, and we could keep ice cream in the freezer portion of the refrigerator. It even had a storage bin at the bottom for potatoes. It took all of us in the family the longest time to call it the refrigerator instead of the icebox.

I don't know exactly when it happened, but I eventually met my best friend, Willie Fairchild. He was taller than me but I was stronger. We became the greatest of pals. Even the memory of Wally began to be erased from my mind. I used to meet Willie nearly every night downtown. Everyone in the town knew everyone else, and it wasn't long until I became a full-fledged member of the community. As time passed, I was able to identify the cars, pickups, or dogs that each family owned. Willie Fairchild was particularly good at that.

We had some pretty exciting things to do that kept us very busy and entertained. We could choose to go into the hotel lobby and play cribbage and look at all the old-time logging pictures. One of the loggers I used to look at and wonder about was Whistling Pete. All the kids said that it was a real treat when Whistling Pete came to town. The first thing he would do was go straight to Olaf Olson's Barbershop and get all clean shaven and have his hair cut. Then he would go to Fairton's Clothing Store and buy a whole new outfit. He would usually buy a beautiful red and black-checkered lumberjack shirt, a pair of stag wool pants, and a warm pair of packs. Packs were red rubber lumberjack boots that I wanted. Every older boy in Littlefork wore them. They always came with beautiful yellow leather shoestrings. After Whistling Pete was cleaned up and dressed up, he would proceed to go on a long drunk. His drunk lasted as long as his money would hold out. Every kid in town would hang around the taverns looking for Whistling Pete; and when they found him, they would try to get him outside where Pete would dish out the money. Willie said that one time he gave him a dollar bill. He said it was one of the greatest days of his life.

Another thing we used to do was to go over to Fairton's Department Store and stand by the display window and look at all the servicemen's pictures. Of course, I didn't know any of them personally. I did, however, learn to know their names and faces through Willie. There were air force pilots, navy and army pilots, gunners, infantrymen, sailors and marines, all with their pictures in the window. Their uniforms were beautiful, and I could never forget their smiling faces.

We used to have a game whereby we could be any one of them we wanted to be; then we would each tell stories about our service experiences. Tojo, Mussolini, Hitler, Rommel, and Hirohito would really catch it. I used to hate those warmongers more than anyone in the world.

All of us would spend hours at that window dreaming of the day when we could finally wear the uniform of our country. Willie had his mind set on the marines, and I was definitely going to choose the navy. Almost every night someone would tell me, "Kirtland, you can't get in the service because they won't take you with your bad hand. You will be 4F for sure. Whoever saw a sailor with only two fingers on his hand?" I used to argue with all the kids about it. Willie used to tell me that he was sure I could get in; maybe I could get an office job or something like that. Throughout our arguments I could never understand how it could possibly be that I supposedly couldn't fight for my country because of my bad hand; yet, I could lick nearly everyone in the group, and I was one of the better basketball and football players, too. I also could run the fastest, but even I was doubtful that they would take me. It seemed as though every reliable adult that I would ask answered the same, "I kinda doubt that they would take you with your hand and all, but you can always do your part here at home. You can help win the war on the home front." Boy, that made me mad.

I still, however, wanted to believe Uncle Sam would have me; consequently, being in the service really occupied a good deal of my thinking time.

One night while we were all standing around looking at the pictures, Willie Fairchild came to join us. He was wearing an army shirt with corporal stripes and an army hat with three gold letters that said, "U.S.A". His pants weren't authentic army but they were khaki in color. He had his pants tucked into his boots like a paratrooper. Everyone looked at him for the longest time. We all thought that Willie had joined the army in spite of the fact that he was only twelve. He was envied by the whole group.

Willie's Uncle Leo used to send him army equipment; and his dad, who lived in Arkansas, also sent him gifts that were the kind of things that we had never seen before. Willie had plenty of "ins" being he had an aunt working at the drugstore and a mom working at the Dusmar Hotel; he had some special privileges that the rest of us could never have.

His Aunt Sarah used to save all the unsold comic books and he would get them. Through his Aunt Sarah he also had a job working for Ed Peterson, the owner of the drugstore. Every once in a while Ed would have some boxes to be moved around and he would have Willie do it. Ed always dropped some pretty good change on Willie; and, as a result, I would profit, too, because Willie always shared with me. With Ed Peterson's money, we would get some pop at Archie's Lunch or ice cream bars at the grocery store. Boy, that Willie was really some friend.

Every other day after swimming in the river, we would go over to the Dusmar Hotel. Willie's mom would invite us into the restaurant portion that was closed to the public because of the war, and then she would fix us a special sundae. I was pleased that she wasn't one bit afraid to put plenty of topping and nuts on our sundaes.

We both tried hard to save what little money we could for our defense stamp books. When we each had a dime, we would go over to the post office and buy a ten cent defense stamp from Mrs. Dobbson, go back to the Dusmar for our sundae, and then Willie's mom would bring us a glass of water; we would then start our ritual. We called this glass of water a Slap-a-Jap Cocktail or Slap-a-Nazi Cocktail because talking like that was the patriotic thing to do. We put the stamp in the water, pasted it in our defense stamp book and then drank the water. There were times when I wished we would spend it in other ways, but we both knew it would bring all the boys from Fairton's window home sooner, so it was worth the sacrifice.

Ending the war and bringing our boys home was what everyone wanted. Each night I would kneel down at the side of my bed and plead, "Please, God, help us end this terrible war and bring our boys safely home."

There were some sad, sad days when my dad would return to the house after meeting the passenger train. "I have some very sad news," he would announce. "Another Littlefork boy was killed in action. I guess he was hit by some shrapnel during the Normandy invasion. His parents were at the depot this morning to meet the body. They were sure broken up," my dad continued.

"Who was it?" my mom asked.

"Larry Stapleton," my dad replied.

My mother gasped, "Oh, my God! I just talked to Mrs. Stapleton yesterday. That poor woman. She's lost her second boy now. I'd better get a hot dish over to the house right away."

I knew that the American Legion would put on a big military funeral and that the parents would receive a check for $10,000 from the government. Mrs. Stapleton would get another gold star for her frontroom window, and she would definitely lead the coming Fourth of July parade. Even though all of this would help ease the Stapletons' pain, it wouldn't bring Larry back.

Fighting the war on the home front became an important part of our lives. We organized a scrap iron drive by borrowing a four-wheeled trailer owned by Marshy Noble's dad; then Dale Anderson, Roger Von Almon, Marshy Noble, Willie Fairchild, the Berg brothers, and I would go around town pushing the four-wheeled trailer looking for scrap iron. Each of us had a rank. Marshy was the general because he had the trailer. The others of us had assigned ranks by General Noble. I was a corporal; that was the lowest of ranks we had. I understood this, as I was pretty new to Marshy. Gradually I worked my way up to staff sergeant; but by that time, the rest were all majors and generals, so I was still the lowest ranking officer. It didn't matter though because we were doing our part, and we were winning the war slowly but surely.

After we wheeled the trailer around for a time, we would all break up and head for the swimming hole on the Littlefork River. We swam above the rapids. It was a beautiful place where the river took a big bend, carving out a deep, deep swimming hole. We tied a big rope to one of the over-hanging branches of an elm tree, and we would swing way out into the river playing Tarzan. We rarely wore swimming suits, and it was some sight seeing everyone running around naked as jaybirds. From the waist up we were a deep dark brown, and below the waist we were as white as sheets.

All of our fathers were civil defense members who met often to discuss procedures that the townsfolk should follow during air raids, possible bombings, blackouts or invasion. It was from those meetings that we were encouraged to develop scrap drives that were designed to end the war and bring our boys home sooner. Marshy's dad was especially patriotic, so it wasn't difficult to convince him to let us use his four-wheel trailer to collect the scrap. It was a beauty! It had nearly new tires and a wooden box with side brackets so that small items would stay on the trailer.

Marshy steered the trailer right or left by guiding the long iron tongue. Two or three of our officers pushed on the sides of the trailer; I always pushed on the rear. We went all over town, up and down the dirt streets collecting any aluminum pots and kettles, scrap iron, worn out pure rubber tires, and newspapers. Everyone in town saved his or her scrap and donated it to us as we covered the Littlefork community.

As we pushed our trailer through the neighborhood, we marched and chanted the marching song that Willie's Uncle Leo taught him when he came home on a ten-day furlough. Marshy, our leader-general, sang the lead sentence and we answered him. I just loved it and felt so good inside working for the good old U.S.A. When there were no people outside of their houses or on the sidewalks, Marshy would start off by counting and chanting:

> Hut Huttle Hut - Hut Huttle Hut.
> Hut 1 - 2, Hut 3 - 4
> Hut 1 - 2 - 3 - 4
> Hut Huttle Hut - Hut Huttle Hut.

When Marshy saw any people gathering, especially girls in our class, we would all chant the part that I really liked best.

Marshy:	You had a good home when you left!
All of us:	Your right!
Marshy:	Jody was there when you left!
All of us:	Your right!
Marshy:	Sound off!
All of us:	One - two.
Marshy:	Sound off!
All of us:	Three - four.
Marshy:	Change count.

All of us:	One - two - three - four
	One - two
	Three - four!
Marshy:	Hut Huttle Hut - Hut Huttle Hut.
	Hut Huttle Hut - Hut Huttle Hut.
	Hut 1 - 2, Hut 3 - 4
	Hut 1 - 2 - 3 - 4

We were all beginning to take some pride in our personal appearances, and our hair, of course, was the most important part. Crew haircuts were beginning to be the most popular hairstyle, especially since almost all the servicemen wore them. We used to try to get Olaf Olson, our barber, to give us a crew haircut, but he wouldn't. Time after time, we told him right to his face that he was a poor barber and that he couldn't cut a butch. He kept saying that he could; but that if he cut one, we probably wouldn't take care of it. He had the most terrible obsession about people with crew haircuts and their not keeping them brushed up.

One day when I went to the barbershop, Olaf finally agreed to give me a butch haircut. Willie was along, of course, and he observed the whole scene. After a great deal of persuasion, Olaf agreed to cut Willie's, too. We were so proud of our butch haircuts as we left the shop.

Whenever we went swimming, we would return to Archie's Lunch for a bottle of pop. We were very careful in avoiding Olaf as we rode our bikes past his barbershop for if he spotted us zipping by with our butches lying flat, he would never have cut us a crew cut again.

One hateful day my father announced that Bill Shawton was coming to town. He was a friend of my dad's from Bemidji and he was a barber. He was intending to open a barbershop in Littlefork, and my dad said that he was going to trade with him. He expected me to do likewise.

Bill Shawton finally opened up his barbershop, and my father was his first customer. When my dad came home, I looked at his haircut; it was obvious that he had received the worst haircut I had ever seen. It looked like Bill put a bowl on my dad's head. I vowed I wouldn't go to Bill under any condition and was surprised that my father didn't really press the issue as I had expected.

Several months after Bill Shawton's arrival, he was invited to our house for supper. When I came home, my dad met me out in the yard with a cap in his hand. It was the middle of summer, but my father insisted I wear the cap so Bill wouldn't see my fresh Olaf Olson butch haircut. I wore the cap in the house; and when suppertime came, I sat at the table wearing the cap, insisting that I didn't want to take it off because I liked my cap so much. Because Bill was so special to my father, we had our supper in the dining room. My mother put out the best we had in silver and china. My dad still believed that Bill represented real class. We passed the various dishes around and Bill demonstrated the manners of a pig. We all sat there in disbelief. He ate his peas with a knife. I had never seen anyone quite so clever in eating peas that way. He would put his knife on the plate and somehow scoop up about ten peas. Then with one motion the peas would be up and in his mouth. It was amazing how those peas rolled down his knife, not one falling to the side. He jammed the food down with such speed that he resembled a pocket gopher. As my dad spoke to him, he would just say, "Umm, hmm, um hm," and continued shoveling in the food. He was a spectacle, to say the least!

After supper was over and Bill left, we all asked my father what he thought of Bill Shawton. "Well," my dad said, "there's lots worse fellows than old Bill Shawton."

After that episode, whenever anyone wanted to jokingly protect anyone in the community, the saying in the family was, "Well, there's lots worse fellows than old Bill Shawton." My father would begin to smile. It was the kind of remark that would bring a smile to my dad's face no matter how serious the situation was or seemed to be. We all used it to good advantage.

We slowly became important citizens in the Littlefork community. My mother was the president of the Ladies' Aide, my father turned Catholic and was chosen to be a member of the parish board and was also selected to be an air raid warden, Lois became a cheerleader, Pat played in the band, and I was the only altar boy. I finally got to carry the incense pot!

The priest, Father Riley, occasionally came to our house for a visit. Doctor Craig spoke to us on the street, and it seemed to me that we weren't the low-class citizens we once were. My dad was putting away a savings bond a month; and although we still had our '31 Chevrolet, things were definitely looking brighter. We, of course, could justify the old Chevy because due to the war no one was able to get a new car.

North of our house, in the opposite direction of the depot, the tracks continued toward International Falls. About a mile up the tracks was a beautiful blueberry patch. It was really our family blueberry patch because it was located so close to us. The only way anyone could approach the patch was by walking through our property. I picked many quarts of blueberries from that swamp; and, consequently, had good spending money as a result of my effort. Probably one of the only ways I could pay Willie Fairchild back for all of the good things he did for me was to take him blueberry picking in our private patch. In this way we could use my house for departing to and arriving from the patch. My mom always had sandwiches ready for us; and, of course, there was water or lemonade to drink.

One day while we were out in the blueberry patch, we decided that with all the dead tamarack trees available to us, we should saw them down, get them up to my house, haul them downtown and then sell the trees for firewood. We planned our logging business out very carefully; Willie was to furnish the saws and axes, and I was to contact my dad to see if he would haul the wood by rail from the blueberry patch to our house. We went around town to take orders from people, and one old widow lady said she would take a cord. As soon as we had that order, we went to work.

The first day's cutting in the swamp was the last. We chopped ten trees into pole lengths and piled them up. We decided to give up on the idea, as it was far too hot. There were too many mosquitoes and flies. Besides, the old swimming hole in the river was beckoning us.

As we rode our bikes past the fairgrounds, Willie said, "Look at that, they are changing the fair sign. It won't be long until the fair will be in full swing. It's always a big event in Littlefork. I sure hope you have saved all of your money."

"Money, hey, I have plenty of it," I said to Willie. My weekly allowance had been really counting up. Yes, I would be very ready for the big fair!

CHAPTER 16
Fair Time

Many interesting things continued to happen the rest of the summer, and I was in the thick of them from morning until night. I had so many jobs I didn't know exactly where to turn or what to do next. My schedule was the only thing that saved me. I followed it religiously because I had responsibilities. Each of my jobs was completed by the personal touch. To me, every animal on our little farm was a complete and unique individual.

We had forty-two chickens and I had a name for many of them. There was a Red, Don, Beryl, Jack, Velma, Henry, Margaret, Aunt Eva, Uncle Fred, Wally, Nancy, Patty, and Joy. I named them after our family, friends, and relatives. I could recognize every one of them. I fed them twice a day. I also dug worms for them in my spare time. I enjoyed digging four or five dozen worms and tossing them into the chicken yard just before going to supper. I used to ring a little bell when it was worm time, and they would all come running toward me rapidly with their wings dropped. On days when friends were over, I would ring the bell to show them how I had my chickens trained to come to me just like students come to school.

Our pigs were really growing. They, too, received a feeding twice a day. I dug a special hole for them and filled it full of water. I used to love to sit on the pig house and watch them lay in the mud hole soaking in their laziness. They really enjoyed rolling and laying in the mud on the hot summer days.

Every morning and night after my dad milked Dinah, I would crank our little one-pail separator. The skim milk would then be split between Peaches, Moonbeam, my dad's steer, and our two pigs named Charley, after my uncle, and Geneva, after my aunt who lived in Texas. I used to throw Dinah's skim milk into the pig pail and then toss in two kettles of ground feed. After fixing this up by stirring it with an old broom handle, I would feed Charley and Geneva. Charley was the bigger of the two, and once in a while I would kick the heck out of him so that Geneva got her fair share of the dinner.

I slowly grew to hate those two pigs and couldn't wait until we butchered them. I was sorry I had named them Charley and Geneva because I really liked my aunt and uncle.

Occasionally our Rhode Island Red chickens would get out of their fenced area and strut around in the pigpen. They used to love to pick at the pig trough and scratch around in the mud. Geneva and Charley would always chase the chickens but they would almost always get away.

One day I came to the pigpen and saw Charley squeezing Henry into the corner of the wire-meshed fence. He was moving his jaws up and down on Henry's back and Henry was squawking like crazy. When I saw what was going on, I ran into the pigpen with a long two-by-four in my hands and hit Charley on the back as hard as I could. Charley squealed so loud that even Geneva ran for the pig house. Geneva went in first with Charley limping behind her. Then I looked down at poor Henry who was just gasping for breath. His whole back was eaten away by Charley and blood was dripping from his wings. I hated that Charley so much for what he had done that I could have killed him on the spot.

Henry died a few minutes afterward. I made a little cross out of chicken feathers for Henry's grave. I placed him in a two-pound Folger's coffee can and buried him in the woods behind the barn. Several months later I dug him up to see if he was still there. When I uncovered the coffee can, I encountered a terrible, stinking mess. It made me so sick I threw up all over the can and Henry's grave.

Yes, those two pigs caused me nothing but grief. I went to feed them one night by scooping some middling from the barrel in the garage. It was nearly dark so I couldn't see too well. I felt down for the scoop kettle; and when I had my hand on what I thought was the handle to the kettle, I felt something furry instead. As I pulled my hand away, I sensed a terrible sharp pain in one of the fingers on my right hand. I looked down into the barrel and there was a big, fat, brown rat. He was so ugly! He had yellow teeth and spit at me while he stood in the feed on his haunches. He slipped back on his back and tried to stand up to defend himself. All I could say was, "Oooh, oooh" and completely lost my breath. I nearly fainted.

I ran to the house with blood dripping from my hand. My mother met me and calmed me down. She called my dad who was close to the house working on the tracks. My dad took me to the hospital, and Dr. Craig gave me some type of a shot and bandaged my hand.

I was so afraid to go in the garage again because of that episode. Charley and Geneva received several beatings for the pain they caused me. My dad put out some rat poison, but I still didn't feel good about going in there. Every time I had to go in the garage, I would take a railroad spike and rattle it around in a pail to warn anything in there that I was coming. While rattling the spike in the pail, I would sing In Nomine Patris, et Filii et Spiritus Sancti. Amen! as loud as I could. I found myself singing Latin prayers in advance of my approach to the garage, woodshed, barn, pig pen and the root cellar. From that time on, I was deathly afraid of rats.

One day I thought I would set a trap for a rat just in case one should try to get in the barrel again. I placed four or five steel traps around the bottom of the feed barrel and nailed the chains of each trap to a large plank.

The next morning I heard my dad hollering and snorting, "Where is that trapper?" My dad came to the stairway and in a singsong fashion hollered up the stairs, "Come on down, Billy boy. You've got a sweet mess in the garage, and I'll let you figure out how to take care of it."

I heard my mother inquire of my father, "What's wrong, Henry?"

And he said, "Well, your little boy has set some traps in the garage, and he has caught himself a skunk that is really stinking up the place. It's all over the car and everything. It's a real sweet mess."

When I heard that, I ran to my window and I could see that I had problems. My mother, dad, and sisters were all standing by the pump a good twenty-five feet away; and there, inside the garage, I could see a big skunk trying to get away. My trap had him firmly by his hind foot. As my dad said, it was a sweet mess. I could smell the aroma way up in my room and the air was blue.

Finally, Art Hegsteadt, one of Dad's men who always got the dirty work, was told by my dad to take care of the skunk situation. I immediately hid under my bed for fear my dad would come and get me to assist Art. I didn't see the whole thing, but I was told it took several minutes to choke the skunk to death. For the remainder of the summer the whole yard smelled of skunk. I was ashamed to have any of my friends come to the house to call on me.

Somehow I managed to lay all of that blame on Charley and Geneva. They paid for it. I quit making them a mud hole and fed them less skim milk; and when I knew my dad wasn't around, I would go in the pig pen and kick the devil out of them. It got so that all of my troubles were taken out on those two pigs.

During the entire summer I had combed and brushed Peaches twice a day. She was growing fast and was the most beautiful animal on the farm. I was getting her ready for the fair which was coming to town. I could see the grandstand from our house. The sign on the side of the grandstand said, "Littlefork Fair, August 26, 27, and 28." That sign served as a good motivator for me to take special care of Peaches.

Every day when I awakened, I would cross a day off the calendar. Every day crossed off meant one day closer to entering Peaches in the livestock competition.

Willie Fairchild and I were hired to work at the fairgrounds. His Aunt Sarah was a girlfriend of the fair board chairman. We received a dollar a day for fixing windows, nailing up the cow stalls, and tarring the roofs of all of the buildings. We figured that we would each have $23 coming by the 26th, and knew that that amount of money would be very helpful toward our having a swell time on the rides.

On the 22nd of August our boss, Warren Johnston, told us that we had finished our work. This, of course, meant that we were four days ahead of what we had anticipated. We had $19 coming to us instead of the expected $23. We decided then and there that what we needed to do was break a few windows for more employment. The next day Warren contacted us and told us that some kids had ruined our work; consequently, we had to go back to the job again.

Finally, the 25th of August arrived. It was entry day!

I had Peaches set to go, and I proudly led her over from our house to the fairgrounds livestock building. She was beautiful to lead and there wasn't much I couldn't get her to do. In fact, I could get her to run with me, lie down, or whatever. I was the first one there and had to wait for the entry clerks for over an hour. Finally they came and Peaches was assigned stall number one. Her registration ticket was tacked on the board above her stall.

Geez, I was proud of Peaches, with one exception, she looked so small in that big stall. I knew, however, she was soon to be a grand champion. It was just a matter of time till the judges looked at her and I would be awarded my prize and ribbon.

After giving her some hay and green grass, I proceeded on toward home. I now had my money from working at the fairgrounds; and with $23 in my billfold, I was one happy boy. As I walked by the other fair buildings, I could see all the entry clerks waiting for the various entrants. The chicken barn, sheep barn, and pig barn made a beautiful sight. "Boy, it is surely a big fair," I told myself.

I went over to the chicken barn to see what was happening, and as yet there were no chickens. There were, however, several pens of ducks and geese. As I looked over the many empty pens, I began to do some thinking. "Why not bring over some of our chickens?" I asked myself. Upon talking with the entry clerk, he assured me that it was fine to do so. He asked me if I wanted to enter a rooster as a single pen or a hen as a single pen, or did I want to enter a pen of chickens, which were four hens and a rooster? I told him I didn't know for sure, but that I would check with my dad and I'd be right back.

Learning that they awarded a grand championship, first, second, and third prize, I began to put my thinking cap on. First of all, to my knowledge, we had the only Rhode Island Red chickens in the area. My dad had mentioned that to me several times. "Secondly," I thought, "why not enter four separate pens of roosters, four separate pens of hens, and four separate pens of four hens and one rooster? That would mean that if I had the only Rhode Island Red chickens, I would get all four prizes for each classification."

By the time I got home, my arithmetic told me that I needed to bring thirty-two of our Rhode Island Red chickens back to the poultry barn. I stuffed five of them in a gunnysack and off I trotted. I made seven trips back and forth with a sack full of chickens. The poultry building finally looked as though it had some business, mostly red business. The clerk wasn't exactly pleased toward the end of my entries, and I could tell he knew what I was up to. He knew there was nothing he could do about it.

Entering chickens was only the beginning. Moonbeam was soon led to the fairgrounds cow barn. I trotted him off, and he occupied a stall in the open stock section on the opposite side of Peaches. I considered taking Dinah but my dad wouldn't let me. I also entered stocks of clover and timothy that I found along the roadside and talked my mother into entering several of her knitting and crocheting projects.

That Thursday was really a tough day, and I believe I had never worked quite so hard at any project. Most of our farm animals were now living at the fairgrounds. Charley and Geneva stayed home. I had considered bringing them over, too, but I had no way to transport them.

Toward evening the carnival folks began to pull into the fairgrounds, and nearly every kid in town was there to watch them unload and assemble their rides and shows. Willie and I walked around the fairgrounds many times with great anticipation of the next day.

While walking by several of the carnival trucks, we were approached by a very nicely dressed man who owned a truck that had "Wild Menagerie" painted on its side. He asked us if we wanted to work for him, and we were thrilled at the opportunity. He took us around to the back of the truck and told us to begin unloading it. Willie and I pulled the tent poles, ropes and canvas off the truck first, and then more of the carnival men came along and began to assemble the tent. As they assembled the tent, we began carrying boxes of snakes and other reptiles into the tent. Several boxes stunk so bad that we could hardly stand it.

We finally finished our work at about 10:00 that evening. When we finally got ready to go home, the well-dressed man gave us each a dime and a ticket to his show. We were both very disappointed in our pay but neither of us dared to complain. We must have worked for at least four hours, and getting to see the snakes we had hauled in just didn't seem like much of a reward. When I looked at Willie, he was almost green in color. I thought it was because he was so angry; but, instead, he was beginning to get sick from the smell of the dead snakes.

The next day I got up at about 5:30 a.m.; it was just turning light. I couldn't sleep all night because of the excitement and also because throughout the night the Art B. Thomas show trucks kept rolling into the fairgrounds.

The first thing I did that morning was to go check on Peaches and Moonbeam and then look at all of our chickens. There were plenty of chickens entered but no Rhode Island Reds, so I was looking very good for a considerable amount of prize money.

This was the day that all of the judging was to take place. I knew that by late afternoon I would be rolling in first place ribbons and a few grand championships.

There were so many things going on. I constantly checked on the chickens, Moonbeam and Peaches; it was important that all of my livestock had water and feed. The ferris wheel was being set up and the various tents were going up which I wanted to see. The grandstand act looked like it might be good, as there were several carnival dogs behind their trailer houses. I really didn't know what to do or where to go.

With my fair working money, I went to the Methodist booth and bought a meal ticket for $10. Willie Fairchild said that this was the only way to go because one really got $12.50 worth of food for $10. It was a good deal. I also knew that once I set foot on the carnival grounds where the rides and sideshows were, I would probably completely lose my head, especially when they opened up the "Golddiggers."

The Golddiggers were little cranes with a bucket. If one could manage to get the bucket over the nickels or grab a silver dollar, one could swing the prize to the drop hole and it was all yours.

As soon as I bought my meal ticket, I ordered a hamburger and two bottles of pop. After my lunch I journeyed on down to check on Peaches and to see if she had been judged yet. They hadn't yet started judging the 4H cattle, so I decided to go down and see how things were going at the poultry barn.

When I came up to the poultry barn, I was greeted by Roger Kelly and Vernon Berg. Both of them were very excited. They told me that I had won all kinds of prizes on my chickens. As I nonchalantly strolled down to the poultry pens, I could see blue, red and white ribbons on each pen. "William Kirtland First," "William Kirtland Second," "William Kirtland Third"--there were lots of ribbons and they were all mine. My mathematical mind computed my chicken earnings to $20.25. After adding the $20.25 with my check of $23 for working at the fairgrounds, less the $10 meal ticket, I had $33.25. I went back toward the cattle barn knowing that I would see a grand championship ribbon on Peaches, for she was my cinch winner. I was hoping that Moonbeam would get a second; but Peaches--well, Peaches was Peaches.

When I approached the stall where Moonbeam was, I looked up above on the board to see if there were any ribbons. I was very disappointed as there tacked to the board was a white ribbon which meant a third. I was not only disappointed but ashamed of Moonbeam. Then Moonbeam looked around at me and I felt so sorry for him. He had done his best; even his eyes seemed to water a little. I was so taken up by his poor showing that I forgot about Peaches. When it suddenly came to me, I left Moonbeam cold and ran down the aisles over toward the 4H section and my wonderful Peaches.

When I got to Peaches' stall, I looked up for the grand championship ribbon but there was nothing there. My entry card was still at the top but there were no ribbons. I looked around at all of the other animals, and there were ribbons above each stall. There was a grand championship ribbon above a calf located on the opposite side of where Peaches was tied. It was a scrawny looking Holstein calf that obviously had no business winning.

When I looked up again at where my grand championship ribbon should have been, I noticed that my tag had some writing on it. I climbed up quickly and pulled my entry tag down so that I could read it. As I took the card down, I thought maybe they had run out of the big ribbons. I looked at the card and began reading it.

I read the statement under "Award" and "Judge's Comments" several times until it finally sank in to me that Peaches wasn't a winner at all. She was disqualified because I wasn't a 4H member. I was so mad at that judge. Had he been nearby, I would have told him so right to his face. I grabbed Peaches' collar and pulled her toward me. She was still the best calf in the barn as far as I was concerned.

I ran quickly down to the poultry pens and took one of the blue ribbons from my chicken pens. In one quick flash I came back, and with a thumbtack I attached the blue ribbon to Peaches' stall. I tore the entry card and jammed it down deep into Peaches' manger. I didn't give a darn for the money; it was the hurt I felt for Peaches that really got me.

Just then Roger came up and asked me how my calf did. "Oh, pretty good, Roger, but not good enough," I said. "She won a blue but should have been a grand champion." I was so afraid that he had seen the comments on the entry card. Roger suggested that we should go to the midway for some carnival activity, to which I quickly agreed, as I was anxious to get out of there.

I began to kick myself for not realizing that there was more to belonging to the 4H than just saying that you were a member. I vowed then and there that it would be different next year. I promised myself I would join the 4H and that Peaches would be a grand champion.

As soon as we got to the midway, I began spending my money like a drunken sailor. I took Mae on several rides and played the "Golddiggers" constantly. I was really after a silver dollar and a large Boy Scout knife. I put nearly $15 in the "diggers" and couldn't get that big prize. The prizes were always buried deep into the dry corn. Once in a while I would get the claws of the digger onto the knife or silver dollar; then the carnival man would holler like mad, "Here's a kid that's got himself a knife." When the crowd would gather around, I would get panicky and nervous, causing the jaws to slip off leaving me a few kernels of corn. It was very disgusting but I was determined.

I ate everything on the midway and rode all of the rides at least four times. I stayed at the carnival right up until they began tearing everything down. It was a sad time for me when the lights went out and the music stopped. When it was definite that the whole thing had come to a close, I journeyed over to the Catholic food booth, as I knew my mother and dad would be there cleaning up. Father Riley, my parents and all of our Catholic friends were still very busy. When my dad saw me he said, "Billy, have you had a good time?"

I said, "Yes, but Peaches lost." He consoled me the best he could. I was really far too tired to argue or care.

About fifteen minutes later, we began to get in the car and drive home when suddenly it came to me that I still had a ten-cent punch left on my meal ticket at the Methodist booth. I jumped out of the car running to the booth.

They were shutting down, too, but there was still time to get a bottle of pop for the ten-cent punch that was coming to me. I asked for a bottle of creme soda and took one swig. I began to get a terrible feeling, and then everything came up. I was so sick my knees were wobbly. I vomited pop, popcorn, cotton candy, peanuts, candy bars, caramel corn, ice cream bars, and hamburgers. My dad jumped out of the car, helped me into the back seat, and looked at my mother, smiling, "I guess our boy had a pretty good time, Margaret!"

I felt into my pockets to check my money supply. On the left side of my pants, in the pocket I rarely used because of my bad hand, was the dime that I had received for working for the reptile man. "At least," I murmured to myself, "I'm not broke."

CHAPTER 17
Sirens

Monday morning came fast and I still felt the after-effects of the big weekend. My mother was quick to get me up so that I could go back to the fairgrounds and get all of our livestock.

After my last trip with the chickens, I saw Willie coming on his bike to meet me. It suddenly occurred to me that he had not been around during the entire fair, nor had I seen him after we worked for the carnival men. He began to tell me about how he had gotten so sick from unloading the snakes for the reptile man that, as a result, he had spent the entire weekend in bed. I felt so sorry for him that he had missed the fair; and so while we moved my stock back to my house, I told him about everything. I'll never forget his eyes and how alert he was throughout the conversation.

He was amazed when I told him that Mr. Peoples, our volunteer fire chief, was going to close the carnival down because one of the barkers at the girlie show was using a siren to attract the customers. We agreed that the carnival people were very smart to use a fire siren, as Littlefork people were surely attracted to a fire or police siren. We both knew how inquisitive they were about sirens because when I nearly burned our house down, every person from Littlefork came out to see the fire and fire truck.

Willie said, "You know, I always wanted to know what happened that night when you caused that fire at your house. I didn't know you at the time, but I came out to see the fire with my Uncle Leo. I felt so sorry for you standing there in your undershorts while the firemen and everyone were running around trying to put the fire out."

It was a warm summer night. My mother and father had spent the whole week painting and wallpapering our house. My parents had painted the upstairs early in the morning and wrapped up the job by painting the stairway.

That night I had to enter my upstairs bedroom by a ladder from outside. When I got home, my parents were gone so I was alone. Lois and Pat were staying overnight with some girlfriends. I brought a malted milk from town along with three comic books. The magazine truck had just come in from Bemidji so I had plenty of good reading material. I climbed up a ladder from outside my bedroom window and settled down into my nest for a very pleasant evening.

I was doing a little smoking from time to time and had two cigarettes that I had taken from my dad's pack in my pants' pocket. After reading several of the comics and consuming most of my malted milk, I decided that a cigarette would go really good. I lit the cigarette. It was a Chesterfield and was pretty strong. I looked at myself in the mirror with the cigarette dangling from my lips, and it was obvious that I was a pretty big-time guy. I could almost inhale like my dad, and I was capable of blowing some pretty decent smoke rings. I blew one up to the mirror; it bounced off and then disintegrated. I was truly happy with myself and especially pleased that this night I could smoke in my room with no worries about my parents. Not only were they not at home; but if they were, they couldn't come up the stairway because of the fresh paint.

Just about the time I lit my second cigarette, I looked out my upstairs window and saw my parents coming up the yard in the old Chevy. As they turned into our yard, their lights reflected off a hubcap that was nailed to a corner of the garage. I immediately became panicky and quickly snuffed the cigarette out in the corner of the windowsill. The cigarette was crushed before they had driven into the garage.

As they left the car and walked up to the yard, they were right below my bedroom window. My dad came up the ladder and stood on the first rung. He said, "Bill, are you home?"

I immediately said, "Yup, I'm just going to bed."

My dad was pleasant sounding and said, "Okay. Good. Well, we're going to bed now. You have a good night. In the morning you can come down the stairway, as the paint should be dry by then."

I said, "Okay. Good night, Dad. Tell Mom good night. I'll see you in the morning." I jumped in bed and began reading my comics again, slowly sipping on my malt trying to save it as long as I could.

While I was reading, I heard a strange noise similar to the sound the train made when it came by our house. But the sound had a different roar to it, one that I hadn't heard before. I read a little while longer and then I smelled smoke. I quickly went to the window and looked down at the sill, and there in the corner of the windowsill was a tiny ball of flame.

Without thinking I ran downstairs with my bare feet sticking to the wet paint. I rushed out into the kitchen for a dipper of water from our water pail.

My dad jumped from bed and said, "What the heck's wrong with you, for God's sake?"

I said, "I think I have a little fire upstairs." I ran with the dipper of water back up the stairs with my dad right behind me.

When I came upstairs, the smell of smoke was much stronger; and my dad said, "Good God! You have been smoking! The whole wall is on fire! Run to the depot and have Frank Fairton call the fire department!" We did not have a phone yet, as the phone company did not want to run a line up to our house.

I didn't wait for any further instructions. I headed back down the stairway, outside and on my way to the depot as fast as I could run. I went past the railroad motorcar house at top gait. All of a sudden I smashed into a push car. I hit the push car with both knees and did a flip over the car coming back onto my knees and feet. My momentum carried me so that I lit face downward into a pile of cinders. When I got up, I could hardly walk; my legs hurt so, but now was not the time to cry about that.

I picked myself up and limped as fast as I could for Frank Fairton's apartment behind the depot. When I got to the

depot, I couldn't see a light in their house. I knew that Frank and Anne were asleep. I didn't bother to knock at their door or anything, but just hurtled my way into their house hollering, "Frank, call the fire department! We've got a fire up at our house!"

Frank rolled out of bed and within seconds had made the call. After making the call, he turned on the light; and I noticed that all I had on was my underwear. I felt real cheap and was afraid that Anne might see me, so I started quickly for the door. Frank noticed that both of my legs were bleeding and said, "Let's take care of those."

I said, "No, I haven't time, as I have to go back home to help my dad."

As I left the depot, I could hear the siren from the fire truck which was on its way from town to our house. I was pleased that they were coming so fast. I started back out for our house and fully expected to see everything in flames but didn't. When I came to the house, my mother was outside in her nightgown pumping water; and my father was upstairs throwing water on the wall. He said he almost had the fire out.

By this time the fire truck was in the yard with sirens blowing and red lights flashing. The firemen were all volunteers and really didn't know all that much about fighting fires, but nevertheless they looked plenty good to me. They came out with their hoses and axes; and before we knew it, they were spraying water on the house. One guy was chopping into the roof while Mr. Peoples was chopping into the wall. They sprayed a lot of water into my bedroom before they decided they had things under control.

By this time the entire town was at our house. I had never seen so many people since watching a parade in Bemidji. There were car lights from the main road down by the depot all the way up to our house. There must have been two hundred cars. All of them drove as close as they could get to our house and then got out of their cars and walked up.

The firemen were really upset, as the cars were bumper to bumper on the road and there was no way they could get the fire truck out if they needed to.

The fire department had a notice in the Littlefork Times the next week urging folks not to follow the fire truck and block the road. They said that if the Kirtland fire had been worse and they had needed water, they would not have been able to have done a darned thing but watch the Kirtland house burn to the ground.

When the people and firemen all left, I came in the house. It was the worst mess. Water was all over our kitchen floor, dining room floor and my parents' bedroom. The entire house had mud tracks all over it from all the firemen going up and down the stairs. All of the wallpaper was stained, and the paint was all smoked up and dirty. I knew my dad was going to kill me. When my parents came downstairs, they saw me sitting at the kitchen table in my shorts. I was so sorry for what I did. I couldn't even look my parents in the eyes. I really expected the worst and knew that I deserved to get the licking of my life.

My dad and mom both came to my side. My dad said, "Let's say a prayer and thank the good Lord that it wasn't worse. After all, no one was killed. We can get the house fixed up. Let this be a lesson to you, Bill. No more smoking."

Willie Fairchild said, "I can't believe your dad didn't beat the heck out of you." I told Willie that afterward as we cleaned up the mess, my dad returned to his old self. I think he was a little sorry he had been so mellow.

Willie said, "Okay, now tell me, what did old man Peoples do at the fair?" I told Willie that the carnival guy told him to get the heck out of there so he could run his show. Peoples said he'd close him down if he didn't quit using that siren; and when the Littleforkers heard Mr. Peoples say he would close him down, they all booed poor old Peoples off the grounds. Threatening to shut the carnival down would be the most unpopular thing anyone could suggest. I mentioned to Willie that I overheard one carnie guy talking to the other, and he suggested that these Littlefork people were the craziest he'd ever seen; they not only had lots of money, but they spent it like wildfire. Never in his life had he seen people so eager for a carnival as this bunch.

"Did you go on the rides?" Willie asked.

"Yes," I replied, "every one, about four to five times."

"What else did you do?" Willie asked. I wasn't sure whether I should tell him or not, but then I broke the news that I had attended the girlie show. I made him promise me that he wouldn't tell anyone about it. He was all eyes when I told him about the dances they did and how they stripped down to nearly nothing.

I showed him exactly where the fun house was and described it to him in great detail. "And you know what, Willie? They had this section of the fun house where you would walk down this ramp on the outside of the truck. And when you would come to a certain spot on the ramp, the ticket taker would press a button and it would blow out air from the bottom of the ramp. Ilene Klefstead and Ernie Berg were walking down the ramp and the guy pressed the air button. Ilene's dress went up around her neck. You could see her pants as plain as day."

"Whose all pants did you see?" Willie asked.

I told him, "I saw Ilene's and Ellen Johnson's and Becky Nelson's and several girls' from Big Falls." We laughed like the dickens about it.

We spent the rest of the day at the fairgrounds looking for money. We scrounged around the entire fairgrounds; I found seventeen cents and Willie found a quarter. We were thrilled at the whole idea of finding the money, and it never occurred to me that the day before I was throwing my money away like a madman. Now, a day later, I worked nine hard hours and found seventeen cents.

When I left Willie, I headed straight home to get my chores done. As I approached the yard, I could see my mother outside pumping a pail of water. The chickens were scattered around the yard scratching and feeding. Dinah was in the pasture with Moonbeam and Peaches. Charley and Geneva were resting in the mud. The whole yard was a very peaceful sight. I was very happy to be living with my wonderful family.

CHAPTER 18
The Big Game

Summers and winters came and went. My routine was well established. There was no place like Littlefork. I loved the town and the people.

As I was about to enter high school that fall, my interests had shifted to sports, especially basketball and football. We had heard all summer that we were going to have a new coach from St. Thomas College who had been named a Little All-American football player.

Willie Fairchild and I practiced football every day at the elementary school grounds. We had an old football that we would throw around. I was the quarterback and he was the end. We would pass the ball back and forth by the hours. We soon discovered that no one could beat us two-on-two, and occasionally we would even take on three others and still beat them.

Finally school started. It was sure good to go back, especially now that we were in a different building. Everyone seemed to have changed so much. We were all impressed with the floors, as they were varnished and waxed to perfection.

Our Frosh study hall was a wild bunch. We had a cute little blonde study hall supervisor who had a terrible time with us. We did lots of weird things, and I led the charge with most of them. Just before she would come into the room, we would, upon signal, in unison, stamp our feet to her walk. The minute she would stop, we would stop. We got so we could do it and still look straight at our books. Then, upon another signal, I would jump up and say, "There goes a blackbird," pointing toward the window. Then everyone would jump up and look out the window. This, of course, made her very angry; and she would threaten to send us all down to the principal's office.

In the dead of winter we would open up all the windows before she came in; and then just before she would arrive, we would close them. When she came into the room, she would immediately go to the radiators and place her hands on them, only to receive a hot reaction. We also broke her pencil and then removed the pencil sharpener. She would head back to sharpen her pencil and discover the sharpener had been removed. She would then continue right on past where the sharpener had been, pretending she hadn't even noticed it.

After all of this, I became known by the faculty as a troublemaker and the leader of all the bad things that went on. Any time there was a problem the principal would come down and take me out of class and proceed to quiz me. If I didn't confess to the prank, he would threaten to remove me from the football team or call my folks. I was in trouble constantly.

I could hardly wait for football to begin. The day had finally come when we were to draw our uniforms. The coach gave us our equipment and also a copy of the schedule. Even though the war was nearly over and gas was still rationed, we were going to have a full schedule of games. Both Willie and I were very excited about our chances of making the team.

The first game was with Northome, there, and both Willie and I made the trip. We got beat 45-0 that afternoon, and neither Willie nor I got in the game. We thought we should have played because we both knew that we were better than some of the sophomores and juniors and almost as good as a couple of seniors.

The following week we were to play Kelliher. We had heard that Northome had beaten them by the same score as they beat us, so we knew we had a good chance against the Dragons.

We worked hard all week getting ready for Kelliher. I was moved from third string quarterback to second string quarterback. The chances of playing second string meant that either I would play if we got way ahead or if we were hopelessly behind. Friday finally came; the field looked super as Tom McAndrew had mowed the field with his horse and sickle mower and all of the sophomores had hand-raked it. Liming the field was the work of the ninth graders, and they had done a fine job.

I was really nervous when we dressed for the game. The coach came around with the jerseys before each game and tossed them to each player. I was waiting for mine, as this would be the first time for me to receive a black-and-orange jersey. The scrubs wore their own gray sweatshirts. I felt he'd never get to me, but finally he tossed one my way. It hit me in the face, and I breathed in the smell of perspiration as the armpit landed right by my nostrils. As I reached for the jersey, I wondered what my number would be. It was 23. It was beautiful, all in orange felt on a black silk jersey. The elbows had double pieces of material. My jersey was the nicest thing I could ever ask for. I slid my jersey on over my shoulder pads and tucked it into my pants. I felt so good inside. I was on the second team and we were playing Kelliher, a team we could probably wax with just a little luck.

We went through our exercises and then began moving around the field in offensive teams. I quarterbacked the second team and I was the only freshman on the unit. The others were sophomores, juniors, and seniors. I felt pretty darned important running the show. Finally after a few minutes Kelliher came on the field. They were whooping and hollering as they came from the dressing room. They were dressed in white with bright green helmets. Everyone gazed at them as they ran by. I was amazed at how small they were. There was only one big guy named Norby who our coach had said all week was the guy we had to stop. But the rest were pretty small. Our confidence shot up. You could just feel it.

All of a sudden the bell rang, and within minutes our entire high school student body came running to the field. There were about 120 of them, as our school had 30 students to a grade. It began to be kind of scary. Several teachers were among the students. They had changed to more informal clothing. I had never seen our lady teachers in slacks before.

Several cars pulled up alongside the road. Dr. Craig, the Baptist minister, and our custodian comprised the adult section. Our coach told us to face the field as it was not right for us to stand and gawk at the crowd. Out of the corner of my eye I could see the junior class officers selling pop and popcorn. I could have stood a bottle of pop; but I knew our coach would go straight in the air if he saw me drinking some, even though I was only a second stringer.

Pete Iverson, the referee, came on the field. He was from Big Falls; a fine guy, he always added class to anything he did and this game was no exception. He brought the captains to the center of the field and flipped the coin for the choice of receiving or kicking. We won the toss and it was then that I knew we were okay. Pete then blew his whistle and we were all sent to the sidelines.

Coach Cazemy said the first team should take the field. They jogged out to their respective positions and the game was soon under way. Pete Iverson blew his whistle and Kelliher kicked off. We battled Kelliher to a scoreless first half and the third quarter saw us go ahead by seven points. It looked as though I wasn't going to get in the game, but I was happy anyway. I was a little afraid I might foul things up and then what would everyone think of me.

After a few minutes had gone by in the fourth quarter, Kelliher's Norby intercepted a pass and ran right over Polkinghorne, our quarterback. Norby went on to score. Polkinghorne seemed to be shaken up a little; and on the extra point try, Norby hit him again, scoring the point.

I began to get a little nervous, as I wondered if Coach Cazemy was going to call on me. Sure enough.

"Kirtland," he said in his deep voice, "get in there for Polkinghorne." I ran onto the field and while doing so, I could hear several of the seniors mumble that we would lose this game for sure. Hearing that comment made me doubly nervous.

Kelliher lined up to kick and I was one of the backs prepared to receive. I said several short prayers, "Jesus, help me. Jesus, Mary and Joseph, don't let him kick the ball to me." But just as I had gasped my prayer, the ball came sailing end over end right into my stomach. I ran about five steps and Norby hit me on the 25-yard line. I had never been hit so hard in my life. How I hung onto the ball I'll never know. My head ached and there were little stars sailing out into the sky every place I looked. I felt a deep hurt on my bad hand and I looked down to see if it was still there. It was all there but bleeding. I finally jumped up and hustled toward our huddle, which was already formed by my teammates. When I went into the huddle, I could smell the perspiration. They were all panting hard. They all looked tired and disgusted. I just knew that they didn't have two cents worth of faith in me.

I called an end around play, which meant I was to pitch the ball to Timonen on a single reverse. I knew it wouldn't go anywhere but I thought I might be able to set up the big play. As I pitched the ball to Timonen, sure enough, Norby came across and smacked him so hard that he nearly fumbled the ball. The Kelliher team was coming tough, and that was just what I wanted them to do. When I went back into the huddle, I could see that Timonen's face was bleeding from a scratch near his eye.

I said, "This time we will do the same thing," to which nearly everyone groaned. "Hey, you guys, Cazemy said I was to run this team, so shut up! Now let's go again on the second hut." I was surprised at what I said to the older players. Again, Timonen was hit by Norby before he crossed the scrimmage line. We were slower in coming back to the huddle. It was now third and fourteen. I came into the huddle and said, "Well, this time it will be the end double reverse." That meant the ball first went to Timonen, and he was to hand it off to our right end Johnson, who came back around on the opposite side of Norby. I said, "Remember, Johnny, carry out your fake and let Norby destroy you because we want him on the ground." I was surprised at my giving Timonen orders.

We broke the huddle and began our play. I dropped back about two steps and pitched the ball to Timonen; he headed straight toward Norby with his head down. Just before Norby was going to hit him, he handed the ball to Johnson who was going the other way. Johnson took the ball on the dead run about five yards deep in our backfield. As he turned the corner, I could see him heading for the sideline. There wasn't anyone within fifteen yards of him. He was on his way for a touchdown. Norby was sprawled all over Timonen, and the Kelliher team was jumping up and down with enthusiasm because they thought Timonen had the ball. For a minute, they had almost convinced me that they were right; but as I looked up the field, I could see Johnson crossing the goal line with the ball held high in the air.

We had scored! There was no doubt about it; we had gone ahead. The score was now 13 to 7 in our favor with just three minutes left to go. I felt proud, really proud; but I didn't say a thing. To my surprise, no one said a thing to me either. I fully expected all kinds of pats on the back, but there was nothing; not one word was said to me by anyone.

Our try for the extra point was no good, but we still led by six points. We lined up ready to kick off. Timonen hit the ball pretty good but kicked it straight at Norby, of all people. Norby took the ball down field; and had he not slipped when he was cutting back on the fifty, he would have scored for sure.

On the first play from scrimmage they gave the ball to Norby. He plowed up the center for an easy ten-yard gain. Three plays later they were on our ten-yard line with thirty-five seconds to go. On the next play the Kelliher quarterback faded back to pass and Norby came over into my area; the pass was badly overthrown and all I could mumble was, "Jesus, Mary and Joseph." I kept saying it over and over again. "Jesus, Mary and Joseph--Jesus, Mary and Joseph." Our captain asked the timekeeper for time, as we had no time clock or scoreboard. That was something I always felt ashamed of because in Bemidji they had a beautiful lighted stadium and scoreboard. He said there were twenty-two seconds left. It was now third down.

Again the Kelliher quarterback barked his signals and I again began to pray. I was asking the good Lord not to let me be the goat as I just didn't want to blow it for myself and everyone else.

It seemed like hours; finally the ball was snapped to the quarterback. Everyone from Kelliher started out around the right end. I knew that if my teammates couldn't get the quarterback on the big sweep, we were done. I was jogging over toward the ball carrier when all of a sudden Norby came heading straight at me. I couldn't believe it. His arms were folded up, and I was sure he was carrying out a fake to lure me toward him. I wasn't going to go for him; instead, I started to pursue the Kelliher quarterback on the far side of the field. Just as Norby turned the corner, I saw a little part of the football under his arm. They were using the same play that we had just used to score! By this time Norby had a full step on me, and he was headed unmolested straight for the goal line. I knew that I had to make the tackle or for sure we would lose the game.

I ran with Norby stride for stride but could see that the goal line was just two more steps away. I decided to make a flying dive at the big fullback. Somehow I managed to get my arms around his legs; as I did, I managed to twist my body enough to cause him to hit the turf. As he fell, the ball came out of his arms; it bounded on the ground and skidded straight into the end zone. It was a fumble! We both began to crawl for the ball.

We reached the ball at about the same time but Norby had the longer arms. Just as he scooped at the ball and began to pull it into his arms, it took a twist and went straight under my stomach. I just let my body cover it and knew that no one was going to take it away.

I waited for a long time with my eyes closed. As I opened one eye, I could partly see Pete Iverson's signal. Then I distinctly heard him holler, "Littlefork--touchback."

At that very moment the gun sounded and I knew we had won the game.

Everyone that was at the game mauled me and slapped me. I was so happy that I threw the ball straight in the air. Just then I was lifted in the air by my teammates; even the seniors were carrying me off the field.

The locker room was a constant blast of noise and shouting; it was truly a pleasant experience for all of us. Out of the corner of my eye I spotted our coach. He was headed straight for me. I raised myself off the locker room bench and jumped straight into his arms. He squeezed the heck out of me and said, "Great game, Son."

CHAPTER 19
Vikings

The rest of the fall was pretty uneventful. About the only good thing we had going was the enrollment of a new kid at our school. He would always inquire of the others as to what had happened to my hand and stomach. Willie would ask me to tell the story, and I would always refuse to utter a word about it. I would say in a trembling voice, "I can't talk about it without going into shock." Finally, Willie would tell the kid that I had lied about my age, enlisted in the marines, and had protected my buddies by throwing myself on a hand grenade in Okinawa. We had some great laughs over that story. We always looked forward to a new kid coming to school and seeing me in the shower room.

For my fun I would tell the new kid to tell Willie that he had heard that his dad really liked to dance. When he repeated those words to Willie, Willie would say, "That's some joke; my dad lost his legs in the Normandy Invasion." We just couldn't wait for a new kid to enroll in our school.

The football season was finally over. We always had a two-week lull between football and basketball seasons. During this time we all got together over at Bergs and shot baskets. They had a large truck gear that their dad had welded to a flat piece of steel, and it was tacked to the backside of their garage. The Berg's hoop was in the alley behind their house; consequently, there was very little interference from cars stopping the games. It made an excellent basketball court.

Right after school we would rush down to the Berg's house, choose up sides, and play basketball for a couple of hours. It was really good for us because the rim was much smaller than the basketball rims in the gym; as a result, we all became pretty good shooters.

By the time practice opened, the basket and basketball were not very strange to us. During our spare time we would sit around and talk about how we were going to State, not as spectators but as players. Oftentimes one or the other of us would play the role of announcer by saying, "Starting at the left forward for the Littlefork Vikings, number 33, Bill Kirtland-Kirtland." The person making the announcement would even try to make the echo or sound of a loud speaker. It was a lot of fun.

Just before Christmas we were to travel over to Williams High School. It was a ninety-five mile trip, the longest one of the year. Taking long trips like that was quite a treat. It was really a special thrill because all of the girls would sign up for the trip, too. We took twenty players, ten for the "A" team and ten for the "B" team. Besides the twenty players, we took about twenty more student spectators. The spectators helped defray the cost of the bus; and, of course, it gave us all a chance to sit with our girl friends.

Before the game, we would have a pep fest put on by our cheerleaders. Usually they would prepare a ten-minute skit which always ran down the opponents we were to play. Then the coach would come out; usually he would introduce the team and give his feelings about how we were going to do that night. During the pep fest all of the boys in the whole school would have a chance to sit with their girl friends.

Right after school was out, we would all run downtown, eat several hamburgers, and walk over to the hotel, and sit around before we would journey back to the school again to board the bus for our respective opponent's town. Waiting at the hotel seemed to be the worst time, as the seconds and minutes just dragged. Occasionally we would get into a cribbage game with Jimmy Ericksen, or we would play spread rummy for a penny a point. It was tough when you lost all of your after-game lunch money before you even left town.

Finally the time would come when we would all board the bus. All players would be allowed on the bus first. "A" team players would get the back seats, and the "B" team, the front seats. It was just an accepted tradition that the seniors would have the very back seats, and the juniors, sophomores, and freshmen worked their way toward the front seats. Each player would sit separately in his seat; when the girls boarded the bus, they would sit beside their boyfriends.

Occasionally there were enough signers so another bus would be scheduled. This wasn't usually the case except at tournament time. I was always very impressed with Blackduck High School because they would bring three busloads of kids. Even their band would go to their games. Usually they had a better rooting section than we did, even when the game was played in our own gym.

This night on our trip to Williams we took two buses because the spirit in the school had really picked up. We had not lost a game in nine contests. I was the leading scorer on the team with a fourteen-point per game average. I was good and I knew it. I was tricky and fast, and I was an exceptionally good shooter. I was cocky as well. I always wore different colored corduroy pants with a baggy colored sweatshirt, moccasins or saddle shoes, stocking cap and a fingertip coat. On real cold nights I wore my new zippered overshoes. On game nights I always wore my black and orange cardigan sweater with my big "L" on the side. I bought it from the Duluth Knitting Mill. I received my letter in football. I wasn't one bit afraid to shoot; however, I tried to be careful so as not to be labeled a "ball hog."

When we arrived at the Williams' gym, the "B" team went down to dress. The "A" team sat on the bleachers watching the "B" team warm up. When they went down to receive their instructions from the coach or while the "B" game was going on, we would step outside behind our bus and smoke a quick cigarette.

In between that time, we roamed around the bleachers trying to make time with the Williams' girls. We engaged in all kinds of cheap "show-off" flirting techniques. We asked them a lot of dumb questions about their town, where they shopped, and what their ball team was like. We told them that we were going to beat them by thirty points. We asked them if they had typing in their school, whether they had more than one teacher, or did they have electricity in their houses. By the time half of the "B" game was completed, we knew their names and agreed to write to one another or to see each other when Williams came to Littlefork for their away game. Our girls would always be upset when we talked to those out-of-town girls.

At the end of the third quarter of the "B" game, we all rose and walked the longest way around the gym floor to our respective locker room. This always brought a cheer from our rooting section. This was the time I walked real "catty-like" and slowly.

After arriving in the locker room, we dressed rapidly and then spent considerable time combing our hair. Most of us had crew haircuts. We passed the ball around, bouncing it and making fake shots at the basket while in the locker room.

Just as soon as the "B" game was over, we would come out on the floor all dressed in our black uniforms with white trim. We were the only players who had white tennis shoes, and we were also the only school who had our last names printed on the back of our warm-up jackets. Mine was inscribed "Kirtland--Littlefork Vikings." Boy, we did look sharp and slick!

By now I had begun to get serious, and I would start having all sorts of butterflies in my stomach. It would seem like an eternity before our coach would nod and we would head back to our locker room for last-minute instructions. It was then that he would name the starters. We all knew who they would be, but we waited for the announcement before we peeled off our sweat jackets.

The coach would holler out, "Kirtland and Fairchild at guard, Noble at center, Anderson and Iverson at the forwards." Then he would say, "Well, boys, this is a tough team. I don't know much about them but run your plays and we should be all right." Then he would shout, "It looks to me like you guys really don't care. Do you?"

Then we would all holler, "Vikings!"

And he would say, "What?"

We would yell, "Vikings!!"

And depending on how important the game was or how excited he wanted to make us, he would keep hollering, "WHAT?"

We would scream, "VIKINGS!!!!"

From the gym upstairs, we could all hear our cheerleaders chanting, "Cazemy, Cazemy open the door, let our Vikings on the floor! Cazemy, Cazemy open the door, let our Vikings on the floor!"

Finally Coach Cazemy would say, "Go get them!" We would break out of the locker room with my leadership. I always had a thing about me as I dribbled the ball down to our end of the court. I used to say to myself that if I missed the lay-up we would lose the game. This night I stopped short of the free-throw line and tossed a jumper-up which swished the net, and with that I had all the confidence I needed.

We all toed the center jump circle, shook hands and the referee tossed the ball high in the air.

By the end of the first quarter, we had a four-point lead; I had eight of our fourteen points. By half time, we had a six-point lead; I had scored six more points to give me a fourteen-point first half. The rest of the points were scattered to our remaining players.

By the third quarter, our point spread had changed considerably and we were dead even. I didn't score a single point but had taken more than my share of shots. I was beginning to worry that I had gone into a cold streak and wasn't sure if I should continue to do as much shooting.

During the fourth quarter, I spent my time feeding Fairchild, who had indicated that he could beat his man to the board any time he wanted. This proved to be a good strategy, as Willie continued to keep us tied. We exchanged baskets during the entire fourth quarter with the game ending in a tie; we went into overtime!

By this time the crowd was very excited, and we were all beginning to develop more respect for Williams High School. We went out to the center, jumped, and Marshy lost the ball to the Williams' center. They decided to pull a stall tactic, as our coach waved us back into a tight zone. I was amazed that he didn't want us to go out after them, but we were obedient. So there we stood with our hands in the air while they played "Alley Oop" with the ball near center court.

With but ten seconds to go, their guard moved into our free-throw area and threw up a jump shot. I went up with him, and he managed to throw it underhanded thus catching me by the arm. The ball went up onto the backboard, bounced around a little and fell in. The referee blew his whistle indicating that I had fouled him and motioned that the basket was good. They were now ahead 42-40 with seven seconds to go. Their star guard was at the free-throw line.

The stillness in the gym was something else. He dipped his knees, let fire, and the ball went off to the side of the rim right into Noble's hands. Marshy threw the ball down to Iverson who took a mid-court shot that fell far short of our basket, going out of bounds for Williams High School. All of the Williams' fans cheered a deafening roar, and it looked as though we were finished. Our first loss was only four seconds away.

The Williams' guard tossed the ball inbounds to his teammate. It was then that I sneaked inside the Williams' guard, stole the ball, and in a backward motion threw the ball up toward the basket. It rolled around on the rim and fell in. At the same time the referee signaled a foul on the Williams' guard. By this time the entire gym was in an uproar. We were dancing around at midcourt, and I did not realize the pressure that was soon to be upon me.

The Williams' coach wanted to put extra pressure on me so he called for a time-out in order that I might get a chance to think about it. We went over to Coach Cazemy who looked more excited than I had ever seen him before. He said, "Kirtland, don't worry about a thing; just go up there and take your time. You can make it." His voice was trembling.

I looked up at the clock and there was no more time. I said, "What happens if I miss it?"

He said, "If you miss it, we will go into another overtime; but don't miss it, as they might get control of the ball on the center jump and then go into that stall again. Just make it. I know you can do it."

By now I began to get nervous. The buzzer sounded and the referee waved us over to our free-throw line. I went up to the ball that he had waiting for me. The crowd began to cheer. Our fans kept saying, "Sh, sh, sh." And the Williams' fans began to jeer. My throat was so dry that I could barely swallow; my hands and arms began to tremble. I dipped my knees and carefully aimed the ball. It hit the front of the rim. I was certain I had missed it, but the force was enough to carry it up onto the rim. The ball took a little right pull and began to go around the rim. It started to gain momentum as it went around the first time. Then when it went around the second time, I knew it would fly out as it gained speed. Then the strangest thing happened. The ball went up onto the flange between the rim and the backboard and stopped. It just sat there still and dead!

The crowd went wild! The referees looked at each other. I looked over to Coach Cazemy and started to walk toward him. He waved me back, and all of the players stayed in their respective lanes. I went back and toed the free line waiting for my second opportunity while the referees used a ladder to tap the ball down, as no one was tall enough to bat it out from the floor.

Although we later learned that the referee should have called a jump ball at the free throw circle, he instead brought the ball back to me and the whole thing started all over again. I took the ball in my hands, a little calmer this time, dipped my knees slightly, and pushed the ball carefully; when it left my hands, I knew it was good. It split the net with a pretty swish.

People from all over the gym came and congratulated me. We jumped around for a long time. I was very happy; however, I couldn't help but feel especially sad for the Williams' players, cheerleaders, and fans who were standing over to the side with tears in their eyes.

We boarded the bus and everyone gave fifteen rahs for Kirtland, fifteen rahs for Cazemy, and fifteen rahs for the team. What a night!

CHAPTER 20
Dad Owed Ed Miley a Favor

We finished the season with an excellent record, and
the talk around the conference was that Littlefork was going to
have a terrific basketball team when all of us ended up as
juniors and seniors.

Every day after school I began walking home instead
of taking the bus. The one-mile walk wasn't that bad, and it
gave me an opportunity to visit with my town friends. We
would all walk down the middle of the street and head for the
Dusmar Café, which was the school hangout. In the Dusmar
we would smoke a cigarette and have a Coke without being
hassled. Few, if any, adults came there; and our teachers and
coaches never made their presence known in the Dusmar.

Spring always brought the laziness out of me;
consequently, I was looking forward to the summer ahead. I
was fifteen now and was in hopes of finding a good-paying
summer job. I was too young to go to work on the track for
my dad, but I heard that the R.E.A. was putting on some guys
and that supposedly one could work for them upon reaching
the age of fifteen. The R.E.A. was bringing electricity to all of
the farms in the Littlefork area. Willie Fairchild said that he
heard that the R.E.A. needed some hole diggers and that he
was going to apply.

That night I approached my dad about asking Orville
Hansen, the R.E.A. foreman, about going to work. I knew that
my bad hand might give me some trouble, at least initially,
because people who didn't know me were always of the
opinion that I might not be able to keep up with the others;
however, I seldom had trouble after I once got the hang of
things. Then they would see the results.

When I began talking to my dad and mom about
applying at the R.E.A., I could see by their faces that
permission would not be granted. I had faintly remembered
my dad talking about how he had worked for Ed Miley, a very

good friend on his mother's side of the family. Ed almost raised my dad during the Depression, as he lived with Ed and Elsie Miley for a number of years. He called it working for his keep.

During long winter evenings, my dad often talked of working on the Miley farm; however, I never found much of the conversation that interesting. My dad reminisced that Ed Miley did it this way, and I learned this and that from Ed Miley. He would say, "Oh, boy, that Elsie Miley could surely put on some feed." I was certain that she could never out cook my mother. It seemed to me that my dad put my mom down just a little when he bragged up Elsie Miley's cooking.

When I said, "I don't know why you are so against my taking this R.E.A. job," my dad attempted to explain the situation to me.

"Billy," he said, and when he started off this way, I just knew he wanted a favor or that he wanted me to like his idea; it was always, without a doubt, a plan that I knew I would have to concede to. "Billy, you remember my talking about Ed Miley before, don't you?"

"Yes, I remember. He's the guy who helped you when you were down and out," I replied.

"Yes, Son, he's the man who your dad owes everything to. You see, Billy, Ed's oldest son Harold has been drafted. He could not get a farm deferment. Ed is in a bad way because he is getting up in years and has no helper now and can't afford to hire one. Of course, if I could leave my work, I'd go down there and give him a hand; but you know I can't do that. What I was hoping was that you would feel good about going on down to Mankato and work on Ed's dairy farm this summer. Help him out. If you do this, I feel it would pay Ed back for all the things he did for me. Elsie will really cook some beautiful meals, and the hard work will build your body up for football and sports this coming fall."

I could see my dad was determined and that there would be no other way. Boy, I hated the idea of spending the summer on the Miley farm. It would probably be very lonesome, and the work, the work would be terribly hard and hot. And the pay--nothing. There would be no friends. "Why me?" I asked myself.

Finally I said, "Okay, Dad, I'll do it. I'll go there and do my best, but what about the clothes money that I would get if I had that R.E.A. job?" My dad assured me that I'd probably get some money from Ed; and that, if not, he'd buy my school clothes. This was some appeasement, but I knew that my idea of a good wardrobe and my father's were two different things.

"Billy, I'm pleased you will do this for me, as this will really help me feel good about paying Ed back for all the nice things he did for your dad." I didn't like having my dad show so much appreciation because it just wasn't like him. I always had a hard time talking to him when he got this way.

School was out so quickly I could hardly believe it. I was happy that I had passed all of my subjects with C's or better. I had almost completely forgotten about my summer work at the Miley farm, when my mother reminded me that she had received a post card from the Mileys and that next weekend Ed and Elsie would be coming up to take me to their farm. Again the thoughts of going for the summer with the Mileys brought back an empty feeling. I thought of getting sick or perhaps straining my back. Two nights before Ed and Elsie were to come, I poured ice water all over my head trying to catch pneumonia but nothing worked. The next day I woke up as healthy as could be with no sore throat or illness at all.

Finally on that summer day in June, sure enough, Ed and Elsie Miley drove up into our yard in their pickup. One side of the pickup was all plastered with cow manure. Ed still had his knobby tires on, and one could tell he had gone through plenty of mud. There were two bales of straw in the pickup box along with several old rusty cream cans. I really began to get sick to my stomach at the sight of Elsie and Ed. "Why couldn't some guy with an ice cream parlor have helped my dad through hard times? A truck driver would have been beautiful, a bartender, anyone but a poor old farmer," I thought to myself. "Cripes sake, why did I have to go?" But the hateful hour had come. My dad was forcing smiles, and he was so kind and helpful to me that it only made matters worse.

My mom had big tears in her eyes and said, "Good-by, don't get lonesome, have some fun and be careful, especially around the machinery. Ed, don't let him operate the machinery unless you teach him really good, and remember he'll give you a good day's work."

"He's a good kid; don't be afraid to work him," my dad added.

The last thing my mother shouted was, "Be careful around the machinery!"

We left our house. I felt empty but it didn't do any good. We were on our way to the Miley 360-acre dairy farm in Mankato, Minnesota.

Ed drove his black '36 Ford pickup. Elsie sat in the middle and I sat on the right side with my arm out the window. My suitcase was bouncing around with the cream cans, and I worried that it might jar open and some of my clothes might blow away.

As we drove down the highway, we left the spruce swamps for sandy soil and plenty of jack pines. Every five to ten miles Ed would spit tobacco juice out the window. Some of the spit would splatter on the window and run back on over the cab. Ed stuttered terribly. He stammered, "Uh, uh, uh, uh, there there there there is a deah-deah-deah-deaher-deer on the side of the road." By the time he got out the word, "deer," it had jumped in the bushes and was miles from the highway. Elsie always let Ed talk it out. I wanted to say the words for him but didn't dare.

Finally, after a seven-hour drive, we reached Mileys. The house was a two-story framed building. It was a bright white. All of the buildings were white including the barn. All around the yard were Rhode Island Red chickens. I knew then where my dad had gotten the idea of getting Rhode Island Reds. The Mileys had three geese and several turkeys. All of the cattle were feeding in a green meadow. Ed had thirty-five cows and seventeen young heifers. He had one big, mean-looking bull. The farm had a blue creek running through the middle of it; and, without question, it was a picturesque sight.

When we went into the house, Elsie took me up to my room. All of the way up the steep stairway, Ed had pounded nails in the wall. Ed's clothes were hanging on the nails, and they smelled of the barn and sour milk. When a breeze blew up the stairway into my room, it was pretty rich and almost always made me want to throw up.

I went to bed that night and prayed for everyone. I really thought I was going to be more lonesome than I was; maybe I was growing up. When I pulled the big comforter over my head, I fell asleep in seconds.

The next morning Ed called, "Ba-ba-ba-Bill, it's ta-ta-ta-time to m-m-milk the k-k-k-cows." I looked out the window and it was starting to get light. I could hear the cows bellowing out by the barn. The roosters were crowing and all the animals seemed to be visiting with each other. It was a pleasant array of sounds. I thought to myself, "Maybe, just maybe this Miley farm would be alright after all."

I came downstairs dressed in my bib overalls, blue denim shirt and boots. My boots were official railroad boots with little round steel toes so that if a rail fell on them they could withstand the weight. They were my father's but they fit me. I thought to myself, "At least they will be helpful if a cow should decide to step on my foot."

Elsie had the table all set. She had a beautiful white tablecloth spread out over the round oak table. There were pancakes on a plate, scrambled eggs in a bowl, sausages and bacon on a platter, and some canned pears in a little cracked dish.

Elsie said, "Good mornin', Bill. Do you want coffee to drink or milk?" When she said, "coffee," I couldn't believe it, for I had never drunk coffee in my life. I felt so adult and couldn't imagine being asked my preference. Although I felt grown-up, I also now felt lonesome. I was terribly hungry, yet a little sick to my stomach. I sure wished my mother and dad were by the table, but they weren't.

170

"Oh, no thanks, Elsie; milk will be just fine," I said. "Boy, Elsie, this breakfast is fit for a king, that's for sure," I added.

"And I'm the k-k-king that w-w-will eat it," said Ed as he turned from the radio he was fussing with. "D-d-did you sla-sla-sleep g-g-good, B-b-bill?" he asked.

"Oh, yes, I did. I just dropped right off into dreamland, Ed. I had a great night's sleep."

"Well, th-that's g-good, 'cuz y-you're g-going to n-need it t-today," Ed laughed.

Elsie said grace and then thanked the Lord for her good life with Ed, and also thanked the Lord for bringing them a summer visitor in me. Elsie and Ed were some kind of Protestants so any words that came to their mind were just fine. In our house we, of course, had our standard prayer called Grace. After grace, we all ate in silence. It was the most food I had ever eaten at breakfast.

After breakfast was over, Ed picked his teeth and fussed with the radio some more. Finally the announcer said that he was coming back with the stock report. Ed reminded Elsie to quit rattling the dishes so that he could hear the report. Then the announcer said, "Hello, out there in southern Minnesota. This weather and stock report are both brought to you by none other than genuine Fiester Hybrid Corn, the corn that gives you greater yields and ultimately produces fatter, meatier cattle and hogs. The temperature today is going to climb way, way up to 93 degrees, so it's going to be a hot one!"

"What did-did w-we d-d-do to-to d-d-d-deserve th-th-that?" muttered Ed.

Then the announcer uttered words like, "Hogs--up two; sheep--down four; feeder calves--up two." I never did make any sense out of the stock market report, even though we listened to it at breakfast all summer long. Each day whether it was going to be hot or cold, rain or shine, whatever the announcer said the temperature would be, Ed would always follow up with, "What did-did w-we d-d-do to-to d-d-d-deserve th-th-that?"

I grew to accept my routine. Every weekday I got up at 4:30 a.m., dressed, went downstairs wearing bib overalls and my railroad boots, and greeted Elsie and Ed. Elsie said grace and thanked the Lord for my being there and her lovely life with Ed. I sat down to a terrific breakfast, listened to Ed stutter through the news, weather, and stock reports, listened to Ed tell me how hard I would have to work, and left the table to go out to milk the cows.

Milking thirty-five Holstein cows by milking machine was a lot of work. Ed told me that the R.E.A. had come through the summer before and asked me how I would have liked to have milked all their cows by hand like he, Harold, and Elsie did. I suggested to him that I would have been a real poor one-handed-milker to which Ed chuckled. Ed showed me how to strip the cows and also get them started. He called it "l-l-loosening up t-the u-u-udders." We also had to wash their bags with a wet rag.

Prior to milking the cows we had to go get them. Most of the time they were right by the barn patiently waiting, but there were times when they were down at the end of the pasture. "Come boss, come boss, milkin' time, come boss, come boss," I'd sing as I marched through Ed's meadow. I always took Prince and Lassie, Ed and Elsie's two collies, and had them help me bring the cows home for milking. Prince was a mean dog, and he would often leap up on the flanks of the cows and nip their tails. I used to switch the heck out of him, especially when he went after Big Mama. Big Mama was the leader of the herd and the gentlest animal you ever wanted to be around. I really liked Big Mama. She was the best milker and by far the most beautiful, kindest cow in southern Minnesota.

Ed used to always ask, "H-h-how mu-mu-much m-m-milk d-did B-b-big M-m-mama g-g-give t-t-today, B-Bill?" Usually I gave her credit for a little more than what she actually gave because of her importance to the herd and to Ed.

Ed also had his favorite animal. One wouldn't have had to be on the farm long to realize that Prince was pretty special to Ed. That dog would always be hiding somewhere, behind the pick-up or in the tall grass by the garden, just waiting for Ed to make his appearance from the house, barn or machine shed.

Upon spotting Ed, Prince would lower his head, crawl along closely to the ground, and advance directly toward his good friend. When Prince would get within twenty feet of Ed, he would speed up; and at full gait he would attack Ed's right boot or pant leg in an attempt to keep Ed from walking. If Ed wanted to play, he would stiffen his leg and pull the snarling Prince along dragging him through the grass while singing, "P-P-Princy, b-bad, d-d-dog; P-P-Princy, b-bad, d-d-dog."

Sometimes they played this game while Ed was trying to carry two pails of milk; however, if Ed were in a hurry or if he were wearing his Sunday best, the ritual was off. Prince understood that Ed wasn't in the mood when Ed would lower his voice an octave and sternly shout, "PRINCE - EASY; EASY - PRINCE," not stuttering one word or syllable. Prince would then make about three or four rapid thirty-foot clockwise circles around Ed. Ed would chant, "EASY-EASY-EASY," each time Prince was in the one o'clock position.

When morning milking was over, we turned the cows out; and Ed would say he was going to the house to check on Elsie. I knew that he really wanted to get out of barn cleaning and also have a cup of coffee.

After the cows were put back to pasture, I would commence to clean the barn. It seemed that they just wouldn't go to the toilet outside. They always had to go in the barn for me to clean. Ed had a big cement-type wheelbarrow. I shoveled the manure into it and wheeled it out of the barn up on top of the manure pile. Once in a while I would steer the wheelbarrow off the planks that were used for the base, and then the manure would spill all over at the bottom of the pile. On rainy days when I fell off the plank, the manure would go right up onto my knees, which would really make me upset.

The first few weeks I found wheeling the manure nearly impossible; but as time went on, I got stronger and stronger and the job became a piece of cake.

After cleaning the barn, I might have cultivated the corn with the tractor and the four-row cultivator, made repairs on the fences, weeded the garden, mowed the lawn, or made hay. Ed had eight acres down the road that he rented for hay. He tried to get three hay crops off that rental land, which meant every spare moment, weather permitting, we were haying. I always sang to the grinding and popping beat of Ed's John Deere tractor. I could sing "There's a Star Spangled Banner Waving Somewhere" just like Gene Autry, my favorite cowboy-singer-actor. "Off We Go Into The Wide Blue Yonder," "Over Hill, Over Dale, We Will Hit the Dusty Trail" and "From the Halls of Montezuma" were other favorite songs that I sang while I was mowing, raking or hauling hay.

For the most part, I liked my work and being at the Mileys. I especially liked driving Ed's tractor, milking Big Mama, and eating Elsie's meals. Sleeping upstairs on those summer nights with the window wide open and a nice, fresh breeze blowing in my face was beautiful. I loved watching all the cows grazing while it rained buckets. Playing with Prince and Lassie after doing the chores was great. Going to town with Ed and Elsie to get groceries and driving to town by myself with Ed's pickup on Saturday or to church on Sunday morning were big thrills and gave me a grown-up feeling.

I never grew tired of visiting or observing Elsie. She was, other than my mother, the most beautiful and kindest woman I ever met. She was what I always thought the perfect farmer's wife would be like. More than once I said to myself that if I ever married and became a farmer, I would have a wife just like Elsie Miley.

Elsie could make the most out of the simplest of things; even the many uses she found for her aprons were impressive. While in the house, she constantly shooed flies from the kitchen table in hopes they would rest on the yellow fly gummy paper hanging from the ceiling. "Shoooo!" she

would yell in a loud voice, quickly opening the screen door, waving her apron, ultimately frightening the chickens off the back porch. Her apron served her well on those hot July days when she cooled herself while resting in the living room rocker. Elsie never needed hot pads as she could remove a pan of fresh bread or a casserole from the oven with her good old apron. Elsie's apron was her container for picking garden vegetables, and she never needed a pail to gather eggs from the hen house. She even tied her apron to the broom handle when she wanted to signal Ed and me to come to the table. I sure did love to see that apron waving in the wind when we were on the back forty. I often told Elsie that the Miley Farm could never operate even one day were it not for her and her aprons. When I paid her a compliment as such, she merely smiled and blushed in appreciation.

The thing I disliked the most was Ed's stuttering, especially when he was downtown. He seemed to be so much louder when he was with his farmer pals downtown. Everyone who didn't know Ed would stop to gawk and laugh. Ed's tobacco chewing and spitting were also embarrassing. Working in the garden was boring and tough, especially when the ground was so hard and the quack grass high. Garden work was almost as bad as picking mustard in the grain field. These jobs were especially miserable when it was hot and muggy which was nearly always the case. Shoveling the manure from the barn was bad, although it got much better as I gained in strength and skill. I used to say to myself, "Imagine me, one of the best and strongest manure shovelers and wheelers in southern Minnesota." Cleaning out the calf pen was terrible. I only did it once, but once was enough. That one time was so bad that I dreaded each day when Ed outlined the day's work. I was so afraid he would say, "M-m-maybe wah-wah-we'd b-bet-better cla-cla-clean the k-k-k-calf puh-puh-pen, Bah-Bah-Bill." Yes, cleaning the calf pens had to be the worst job of all.

A month or so after I arrived, Ed's neighbor, Adam Schmidt, came over in his Model A and began to coax Ed to go to town with him. I didn't know it then, but later Elsie told me that whenever Adam came by to be sure to let her know immediately as Adam was a very bad influence on Ed. She told me that one time Adam took Ed to Minneapolis and they stayed there on a three-day drunk. It was tough on her and the farm. She said, "I wasn't sure he was ever coming back," until that Monday evening about milking time she heard the sound of Adam's Model A out in the yard. When she came running from the barn, Adam's car was leaving the yard and there stood Ed. She said that although she was terribly happy to see him, she didn't talk to him for seventeen days; and to this day, she hadn't discussed the details of that fling.

Just before Ed and Adam left for town this time, Ed said, "I w-w-want you t-to g-get the k-k-calf p-puh-pen all k-kla-cleaned up, Buh-Bill." So I went to the barn and started cleaning the pen with a pitchfork. It hadn't been cleaned for a long, long time. The calves backs were beginning to touch the hayloft floor. It was a terrible job. I was sure that Ed, or even my dad, when he worked for Ed, had never cleaned it.

I could have cried. I wanted to hitchhike home. Did it ever stink! It got so bad that with each forkful I would throw up. I started to get the dry heaves. To this day I don't know how I did it. I vowed then that I would never ever be a farmer. I couldn't, for the life of me, understand why Ed had waited so long to clean that pen.

Later that day Adam dropped Ed off. Ed was drunker than a skunk. He staggered all over the yard until he finally made it into the house. Elsie was crying and carrying on. She really chewed Ed out. All night long I could hear Ed throwing up and coughing. Again I wanted to pack my bags and go home.

The next morning the radio announcer said, "Hello there, folks. I hope you're having a good day. She's going to be a hot one today. That old mercury is going to go right on up to 94 degrees. Now what do you think of that, all of you out there in southern Minnesota?"

Ed said, "What did-did w-we d-d-do to-to d-d-deserve th-th-that?" and snapped the radio off. I wanted to say, "You mean `you', Ed, not `us'. You're the one who got drunk yesterday." We all ate breakfast without saying a word to each other.

The Miley's phone broke the silence. It rang three shorts, which I was sure meant that Mrs. Novak up the road was calling Elsie. Elsie said, "Hello, this is Elsie Miley. Yes, oh, it's good to hear your voice. Yes, he's working hard. Oh, we are sure enjoying him." I stopped eating my bacon and thought to myself, "That must be my mother." Then Elsie said, "Bill, it's your dad on the phone up in Littlefork. He wants to talk to you." My eyes immediately began to water. I could hardly contain myself when I went to the phone.

I held the earpiece tightly to my left ear. "Hello, Dad?"

My dad said, "Bill, I need to keep this short, as we aren't talking over the fence, you know. Coach Cazemy is starting football Monday, and he told me that you should be at practice. So take the bus to Bemidji and then the train to Littlefork. Can you hear me? What do you say to that?"

One million shivers went up and down my body. Good old Coach Cazemy! "If he were here by me, I would hug him," I thought to myself. "Dad, I'll explain things to Elsie and Ed. Tell Mom I love her, won't you?" I was so very, very happy.

I looked at Elsie and Ed and said, "I'm going to have to go home."

Elsie grabbed her handkerchief and began sniffling as she ran to her bedroom.

Ed stuttered, "What did-did w-we d-d-do to-to d-d-deserve th-th-that?"

Although I was happy to leave, I also had much sadness in my heart. When I finished packing, I came down the stairway. Elsie was there to meet me. She gave me a long hug. Ed slipped me a check for $200 and said, "That ought to h-h-help you f-f-for sch-school clo-clo-clothes, B-B-Bill!"

Immediately I decided that cleaning those calf pens was worth it, as I had never experienced receiving that much money in my whole life.

As Ed took me to Mankato in the pickup, I looked behind me with mixed feelings. Elsie was wiping her tears with her white apron, Big Mama was in the meadow with all of the cattle, and the chickens were all running for a swarm of bugs that were hatching down by the pigpen. Prince and Lassie barked and pretended to bite at our pickup tires as we headed out of Ed and Elsie's farmyard.

CHAPTER 21
Halloween Boys

School started and it was good to be back again. Our football team was really rolling. I was the starting quarterback.

One night after football practice while in the locker room, a few of us started talking about Halloween. Halloween was really something in Littlefork. Every time the opportunity presented itself, we would sit and talk about the many things we were going to do and to whom. We sort of felt like it was legalized vandalism. Most of the guys were able to reflect on the past and the stories would really unfold. It was great sport to sit and listen to their old experiences.

Roger Kelly said, "Remember when we took old man Warner's hay wagon and pulled it down Main Street and parked it square up in front of the Dusmar Cafe?" Then everyone would laugh about how old D. J. Appleton would cuss and swear, and then would have to call old man Warner who would bring the tractor to haul the wagon back to his farm.

"And remember when," Fairchild added, "we took Maggie Appleton's outhouse clean off the foundation and hauled it to Main Street?" Everyone laughed heartily again.

I really enjoyed all of the stories. Willie and Roger again assumed leadership. I was most anxious to be a part and asked them what the plans were this year when Halloween would come. Willie suggested that this was the year that we should get Hermanson, as he was the old junior high coach who didn't know a darned thing about any type of coaching. He was also the teacher who did some pretty heavy slapping in our junior high math classes. He was the one who would say before class started, "Do you have all your tools with you today?" The tools were your compass, pencil, protractor, paper and math book. He really got ticked off when people would constantly ask him if they could return to their homeroom desk because they had forgotten one of their tools. He obviously had received plenty of scolding from the principal for letting people out of class to roam the halls looking for their tools.

At first when he'd pop the question, "Has anyone forgotten their tools?" a number of people would raise their hands; and then he would proceed to walk down the aisles throwing haymakers at all who had their hands in the air. It became quite a challenge to all of us before class to see who dared to raise his hand. Occasionally Roger would put his hand up and then down the aisle Hermanson would come ready to put his lights out. Just before he would start to swing, Roger would shout, "I have my tools. I was only wondering if you would help me with the third one in row four." Then the class would all laugh and laugh, while Hermanson would run around the room grabbing and shaking the person who laughed the loudest and the longest.

One day Willie Fairchild made a two-bit bet with Marshy Noble that he was going to confess that he had forgotten his tools. I was scared to death for Willie, as when we entered the room it was obvious that Mr. Hermanson had had a pretty tiring weekend. You could always tell when he was especially crabby as he still had some sleep left in his eyes. Another sign was his hair was unmanageable, looking like he had washed it the night before and had slept on it wet. That day he obviously plastered a lot of Vitalis on it, attempting to slick it down. I predicted to myself that these differences in his appearance meant that he was going to be plenty short with all of us.

Yes, this was one of those mornings when Hermanson looked especially mean and tough. But Willie had to go through with it as he had made the bet with Noble, and everyone knew of it.

We all assembled in class very quietly and sat there waiting for our teacher, Ted Hermanson. Finally the big heavy man, who stood at least 6' 3" and was by far the tallest person in the entire school, came into the room. He seemed to sense there was something about to happen and was ready to meet the challenge.

He stood at his desk, took roll from his seating chart and then said, "There wouldn't be anyone who has forgotten his tools today, would there?"

All eyes peered toward Willie. I wanted to cry for him. To Willie Fairchild, losing the two bits wasn't the problem; it would be the constant harassment by everyone. "We thought so; we knew you didn't have the guts," they would say. Either way, Willie was in a bad way.

There was a long silence. I thought that he must have decided not to go through with it. I was relieved for his sake and vowed I wouldn't say a thing to him. Then Hermanson sang, "Well, I find that hard to believe. Surely someone has forgotten his tools."

Then all eyes peered at Willie again. He wasn't able to take it any longer, as he slid his hand slowly into the air and said, "I don't have mine." Hermanson looked stern at first, then actually amazed at the fact that Fairchild had the guts to raise his hand.

Hermanson started down the aisle at a pretty fast pace. Willie was going to get it! There was no doubt about it. As Hermanson approached Willie's desk, he began to go into his backswing and it looked historically as though it would be his most violent hit. Just as he was about to deliver the blow, Willie ducked. Hermanson swung with such a force that his arm and clenched fist continued the follow-through, catching Maggie Farber on the side of the head. Maggie took both of her hands and covered the side of her face. Her ear and face were a deep red. All of the students in the classroom were as stunned as Hermanson. The silence in the room was broken by the soft sobs of Maggie. Mr. Hermanson lifted Maggie from her desk and walked her out of the room. Maggie didn't come back to school for two days; and when she did, he openly apologized to her in front of the entire class. He never did ask the class whether their tools were in their possession again. In fact, he became quite withdrawn. He left teaching that spring and took a job with the bank.

Willie always felt somewhat responsible for Maggie's blow. This had to be partly why Hermanson was to be his Halloween target.

Roger, however, countered with the idea of attacking Olaf Axelton. Olaf was our superintendent of schools and was the chief policymaker. "He was dipping into all the funds, wasn't he?" asked Roger. And besides, Olaf Axelton had personally confronted Roger many times. It was obvious that Roger was the dominant figure in the discussion. Yes, it would be Olaf Axelton, superintendent of schools, who would receive the Halloween treatment for this year. Besides, the school could also be a part of the target; and whatever we did to Olaf, we did to the school.

Olaf never really did that many bad things, except he seemed to enjoy dressing down students verbally in front of other students. He enjoyed walking across the assembly room and singling out certain students as he passed through. He always preceded his message with the words, "Hey, ya." He would be limping along with his head down and would stop dead in his tracks and say, "Hey, ya, Kelly, get to work!" Olaf's buzzing around the school was such common practice that many of the male students would find it good fun to impersonate him. Roger was the best at it. He could mimic Olaf perfectly. He did it so often that several times Olaf caught him in the act. Olaf would really come down hard on him. It was for this reason that Olaf was always out to get Roger Kelly and Roger was excited about any chances to return the favor.

Halloween finally arrived and we all met at the Dusmar Cafe. Marshy Noble, Willie Fairchild, Bob Von Almon, Roger Kelly and I made up the group. Kelly ran the show right from the start. He said, "We will trick-or-treat for UNICEF first. We can make ourselves look like good guys and keep the money; besides, it is far too early to get into the real hard-core pranks. That will come later." And then he added, "I have it all planned out for Olaf."

So we went out trick-or-treating for UNICEF. We knocked on doors and got what we could. Several people commented that they thought we were too old for that sort of thing. Obviously they were like me and didn't even understand what UNICEF was. In almost every case I could tell that the people weren't very pleased with our begging-type tactics. We did not go to Olaf's house, but we did hit every teacher in town, which turned out to be our downfall.

Finally Roger had had enough and said, "It's plenty dark enough now and most of the small kids are off the streets. Let's go over to the school grounds and I'll tell you what I have in mind." He slipped a sack out from under his shirt and inside was a list of things he had planned for us to do. He also had all the necessary items that were needed, plus a map of Olaf's yard. All of Olaf's outbuildings were marked out. There was no question but that Roger had done his homework.

The first thing we did was tip over his toilet. We did it in such a manner that we eased it down so there would be no noise. Fortunately his can was far enough away from his house so that I could see I had a good chance to get away should he hear us and come running outside. I knew, too, that I was the fastest runner so at this stage I was completely comfortable.

Then we took his daughter's sled, Olaf's snow shovel, and his wife's wooden clothes rack, and headed for the school.

Kelly dug some stiff wire out of his sack. With his pliers, we wired the sled, shovel and clothes rack to the chain on the flagpole and all of us started pulling. All of the items went up alongside the fifty-foot pole with absolutely no difficulty. It was an awesome sight; and when everything got near the top, we wound the chain around the catch at the bottom. We began to laugh and roll around on the ground. My stomach hurt from all the laughing. I hadn't had such a good time in years. Roger, with a stern look on his face, said, "C'mon, we're not near finished yet."

"Geez, I thought this was it," I said.

But Kelly said, "Nope."

"What's next?" we all asked in unison.

"You'll see," Roger said. We headed back toward Olaf's house with Kelly in the lead. I was last and began to get a little apprehensive but trailed along nevertheless.

When we arrived at Olaf's house, Roger took two bars of soap from his sack and told Willie and Noble to soap all of the windows on the house. "Don't bother the lighted kitchen windows," he said. I was so happy that Willie and Marshy were selected for that job. We watched them from the ditch by the road as they strode up to the house. "Get the screens, too," Roger whispered. "It's hard to get off the screens." They finally came back with the job done. Bob Von Almon was selected to go to the screened front porch. Roger told him to print, "Olaf is full of Bull", right across the front porch. Just at this time we could see that a person was moving in the kitchen. It was Olaf, and I was petrified! He had on a plain shirt and a pair of old overalls. It was funny to see him dressed in that garb, as he always wore a suit with a shirt and tie.

Finally Bob came back with the job completed. I said, "Let's get the heck out of here!"

Roger said, "No, we aren't quite done, as we have one more job to do. Kirtland, take this thread and pin it to his back screen door."

"Geez, Kelly, that's right by the kitchen, and he's in there big as life," I said. Everyone looked at me; I knew that in order to save my face I had to do it. I took the safety pin that was all ready to go, thread attached, and headed for the back screen door. My heart was pounding like a jackhammer. I crawled the last ten feet and slowly crept up onto the back porch. I attached the pin and ran back faster than I had ever run before. I ran with a great feeling of accomplishment.

Kelly took a piece of hard resin and began to rub it on the thread. "What's he doing that for?" I asked Noble. What I didn't know was that it was making a big screeching racket up on the porch. I never knew scientifically what caused it, but, regardless, Roger was doing a terrific job and making an awful racket.

We were all secluded in the ditch at the end of Olaf's property. Roger said, "When he comes out onto the yard, for cripes sake hold your ground." Within seconds the porch light came on and Olaf opened the door.

"Geez," I said to myself, "he'll catch us sure as the dickens. What will my folks say?" All kinds of things went through my mind.

Olaf looked over the whole back yard from the back porch. We could hear him suggest to his wife, Holly, it must have been their cat in a fight. Fortunately, he didn't see the soap writings on his screens. He closed the back door and sat by the kitchen table. He was eating a piece of pie.

This was really turning out to be fun, and we began to snicker while we were hiding in the ditch. Roger said, "Are you all ready?" There being no response, he began rubbing harder on the thread again. You could almost see Olaf asking Holly what she thought the noise was, and within a few seconds he came out again. This time he had a large five-cell flashlight which he used to scan the back yard.

Now I was scared! My heart was pounding as I attempted to peek through the tall grass. Olaf stood on the back porch and shined the light around the yard. He walked out into the yard in the opposite direction of us looking all over with his light. Then he started in our direction flashing his light into the grass. It appeared he was fully intending to come straight toward the ditch. I started to get up, ready to run, when Kelly breathed, "Not a soul will move." Kelly was tough and we knew that he meant what he said.

Just about the time when Olaf was close enough to flush us out of the ditch, Holly came to the back door and said, "Honey, do you see anything?"

"No," Olaf said, and he turned around and headed for the back porch.

Then the two of them went into the house again. In the process of searching the yard Olaf had inadvertently broken the thread, so it looked like we were finished, which made me very happy. Everyone, including me, indicated that it was too bad that the thread broke because this was just getting to be fun.

Then Roger said, "Well, I have some more in my sack."

I had to think quickly and then said, "Gosh, Roger, I'd sure like to stay, but my dad said I had to be in by 11:00. I'll bet it's way past that now; remember, there's football training, too, you know."

Everyone, with the exception of Roger, wanted to leave, too. I was very happy that Kelly seemed to understand our need to quit, and I breathed a sigh of relief that it was all over.

On the way to town we laughed heartily! We talked about what it would be like the next day in school, and each of us predicted Olaf's reaction to the flagpole. I went home quite proud of my bravery and accomplishments.

When we arrived at school, we stayed our distance from one another. That was the plan so as not to give ourselves away. All of the country kids found the flagpole scene rather amusing. Several times I wanted to take the credit but felt that unwise. In agriculture class Mr. Wilson commented that he had a bet that the five of us had done the dirty work, as he had remembered his wife saying that we were together trick-or-treating at his house. We all denied it, of course, but he said, "Don't kid me, you guys are the culprits."

By second hour I was getting a little more uneasy and began to wish I hadn't had a part in it. When we were halfway through our English class, there was a knock on the door, and sure enough it was Olaf's secretary. She said, "Mr. Axelton wants to see Marshy Noble, Bob Von Almon, Willie Fairchild, Bill Kirtland, and Roger Kelly. He would like these people in his office immediately."

"Oh, boy," I thought to myself, "we are all dead in the water. What will my folks say?" On the way down the secretary stayed right with all of us, so there was no chance for us to talk to each other and decide upon what we were going to say or do. I couldn't believe that with all of our plans we hadn't thought about a story that we could all stick by.

When we arrived at Olaf's office, he was there to greet us at the door. Olaf said to all of us, "I suppose you young gentlemen know that you are in some pretty serious trouble, don't you?" I developed a look of complete astonishment and was sure everyone else did the same. Olaf told his secretary to sit with the four of us while he had a conversation with Bob Von Almon. He said to his secretary, "Let me know if they say a word to one another." Von Almon wasn't in there longer than three or four minutes when Olaf came out and said, "Mr. Von Almon had some pretty interesting things to say. You sit down over there, Mr. Von Almon. Mr. Noble, let's hear your story. Come on in, Mr. Noble." I knew he meant business when he started that "mister" stuff, as he always called us by our last names.

All we could hear from his office was muffled sound. In less than two to three minutes Olaf came out of his office and said, "Well, you Halloween boys can all come in now." We all filed in, just knowing that Noble had spilled his guts all over the table. I could see that Kelly was just fuming.

Olaf said, "Well, boys, it's all over. I now know what you did; and I know that boys can be boys, so I'm going to go lightly on you this time." It was obvious that Von Almon and Noble had told everything; but by the tone of Olaf's voice, he didn't seem to be that angry, which made me feel pretty good.

"I'm going to let you boys decide on what you intend to do about this matter." Then he looked square at Fairchild and said, "Do you have any ideas, Willie?"

Fairchild said, "Well, I was thinking maybe we could clean the whole thing up. You know, wash the screens, put the toilet back and bring back your stuff."

I jumped right in and said, "Maybe, Mr. Axelton, we could rake your lawn to make the whole thing up to you."

Olaf said, "That seems reasonable enough. I'll see you all at 3:30 at my house; and when you leave the school, you can take the flagpole items back to my house. You can continue each evening for an hour or so until you get everything done. How does that sound?"

We all agreed that this was the fair thing. Only Roger seemed to be hesitant; yet, he didn't disapprove of the contract.

On the way upstairs, Roger cornered Bob Von Almon and Marshy. Both of them swore on their church honor that they hadn't said a thing about it. In fact, they said that Olaf didn't even discuss the pranks, but instead he talked about our fine parents and what we intended to do after we finished high school and that sort of thing.

Kelly said, "Why you saps, we've been had! He tricked us! Don't you see? We admitted the whole thing and he didn't even know!"

Just then Mr. Wilson came around the corner with a big smile on his face and said, "And how are you Halloween boys today?"

Kelly vowed then and there to himself and to all of us that Wilson would be the Halloween target for next year.

CHAPTER 22
Final Toot-Toot

It was very, very late. All of us were exhausted. My mother's eyes were red. Throughout the evening we had many laughs and cries. As I started up the stairs for bed, Pat said, "Bill, what were you and Uncle Charley talking about for such a long time?"

"I'll bet you were discussing our Christmas trip to Texas in '43," mused Lois.

I laughed and said, "Yeah, wasn't that something, that trip to San Antonio; both Uncle Charley and I really got a kick out of talking about that visit."

My dad brought it up that summer when the blueberries were ripe. He said, "Margaret, I don't know about you and the kids, but I'm saving all of my extra money to go down to Charley and Geneva's for Christmas. You folks can do what you want with your blueberry picking money, but I'm going to use mine to get out of this frozen North Country and live a little."

And so it was, we were going to San Antonio, Texas! Somehow we would manage; we had plenty of blueberries to pick, our railroad passes would get us there, and my dad was entitled to two weeks of paid vacation time.

So that summer we picked pails of berries. Just as soon as my dad came home from work at 5:00 in the afternoon, we would leave for our private berry patch. I would have all the chores done, my mother would have sandwiches packed, and we would all head for what we called the Kirtland Gold Mine.

We would carry our gallon pails along. I always carried an extra kettle in case we ran into some real good pickings. My dad had all of the mosquito and fly dope. Lois carried the big thermos full of lemonade or Kool-Aid, and Pat helped my mother with the lunch. We had our picnic supper in the blueberry swamp.

After our picnic supper, we picked for about three hours or until our pails were full. Then we would walk back up the tracks for the house, load up in our Chevy and head for town. We sold our berries to Ernie Reimerson who owned one of three grocery stores in Littlefork. Ernie paid very well and always gave us a good measure. Following the sale of our berries we usually bought a six-pack of strawberry pop and a quart of Land O' Lakes Vanilla Ice Cream to take home for our treat.

When we arrived home, we salted our money away in our special containers. I was especially impressed with my father's two-quart fruit jar and wondered if he would ever fill it. Each night we would tally our new earnings and place the amount gained on our accounting slips that were kept in our respective banks. After we straightened out our finances, we would proceed to make ourselves a strawberry pop float and then talk about the winter coming on with Christmas in Texas.

By fall, with the blueberry picking season over, our money earning projects had changed. Lois and Pat were picking up their money from babysitting, my dad gave me an allowance for caring for the animals, my mom took in ironing from two bachelor teachers, and my dad became the caretaker of the potato warehouse down by the depot.

Frank Fairton helped Dad set up our train schedule and ordered our passes. My dad brought home an old map of the United States that Frank gave him. We plotted our trip from Minnesota down to Texas. Each night we discussed the states we would travel through, eating pecans on the grass in Uncle Charley's back yard in December, our behavior while riding the train, the possibility of eating one meal in the dining car and on and on. I never grew tired of our nightly discussions and sessions about our Texas trip. It was wonderful to sit around the barrel stove in the living room each evening. I could tell that everyone in our family was very excited and happy.

I didn't think the day would ever come for us to go, but it did. We boarded the train at 7:29 in the evening with all of our winter coats, overshoes, a huge lunch of sandwiches, fried chicken, and our big thermos full of coffee. We had shopping bags full of items that would be needed while on the train. Our suitcases were all tied with clothesline because the locks were broken. We had a huge black trunk, which was checked and loaded in the express car. It was to go straight to San Antonio without our having to carry it. It was filled with potatoes that my dad bought from the manager of the potato warehouse. "Uncle Charley, Aunt Geneva, Cousins Glen, Jack, and Johnny don't get to eat white potatoes that much, since farmers in Texas don't raise that many," my dad said.

As the train slowly left the Littlefork Depot, we were all very excited. My dad winked at me and said, "Billy, just remember there are lots of people in Littlefork who would give their eye teeth to be going with us." Then he turned to my mother and said, "Don't forget to get this in the Littlefork Times, Margaret," He sat back, opened his wallet and hummed, "Look at all of this blueberry-picking money, ah-ha, 'San Antone.' "

When we boarded the train, we were pleased to see that our Uncle Oral was the conductor. He was my dad's older brother and was most happy to see all of us. Shorty Oftedahl was the brakeman so it was old home week until we got to Bemidji. It was surely good to hear about all of our friends in Bemidji, especially our neighbors who lived in Mill Park.

When we pulled into the Bemidji Depot, my Grandma Schmit was there to meet us. We loved her and hugged her, but didn't visit too long before the train pulled out to head south for Minneapolis and St. Paul. As we rode out past the depot, I shielded my eyes in the train window and could see the bridges where I used to play. I almost caught sight of my piling where I caught the big Northern Pike, and then we slipped past Mill Park. We all saw our house up on the hill. My dad said, "Boy, I'm sure happy we're not living there anymore," to which none of us responded. All night long the train groaned and moaned and said, "Clickety-clack, clickety-clack."

We pulled into St. Paul the following morning. We had an eight-hour layover before our train was to leave for Kansas City, Missouri; so, as planned, we took a streetcar out to "Monkey Wards." I could not believe the size of that store! I always heard that it was huge, and I dreamed about going there when I would sit out in the outhouse gazing through those old "Monkey Wards" catalogues. I always wondered if it was possible to have a store where all of that merchandise was on display. I found out. We spent the entire six hours there and had something to eat in the cafe section of the store. We all spent some of our money, but my dad constantly warned us, "Be careful, we've got a long road ahead of us." Riding the streetcar back to the St. Paul Union Station was really something. My dad said, "There are Littlefork kids that will never be this lucky."

We boarded the Rock Island Railroad that evening for Kansas City. The Rock Island cars were not as nice as the Northern Pacific, but the train had a diner and bar car. Every so often my dad would go back to the bar car and get a whiskey drink. I was so afraid he might get drunk and spend all of his money or that someone might hit him on the head and steal it from him. I didn't dare offer him advice. I had to admit that when he returned from getting a drink or two he seemed to be friendlier and happy-go-lucky.

There were many servicemen on the train, so in order to make room, I had to sit with three sailors. At first I thought this was a real treat. When they started drinking and swearing, I began to worry that my mom might hear them so I was uneasy much of the way. I tried to get some sleep but they were loud and boisterous, telling jokes all night.

In the morning the youngest sailor of the group named Bruce, who came from some little town in Mississippi, showed me his tattoo on his arm. The tattoo was a Hawaiian hoola dancer. He could make her dance by pulling on the skin on his arm. I had never seen anything quite like it and wished that my mother wasn't sitting so close so that I could get a better look. I wanted to ask him if he thought I could get into the navy with my crippled hand, but didn't dare.

We finally pulled into Kansas City that morning and had to run like the dickens in order to catch our train for Texas. We ran through the huge station and boarded our train which left minutes after we were in our seats. Our new train was called the Katy Flyer; it was the Missouri, Kansas, and Texas Railroad. It was a long train with fifteen cars.

My dad said that traveling from Kansas City to San Antonio would be the longest part of the trip. He said we would be riding for two days and two nights. I really couldn't understand where the train got its name, Katy Flyer, as we stopped at every town along the way. Many, many times we had to leave the main line for the sidetrack in order to let the more important trains go by. Most of those trains had two or three sleeping cars, bar cars, dining cars plus many nice looking coaches. Slowly, I could see that we were traveling on just an old milk train.

My mother placed our sandwiches, fried chicken, pickles, cookies and cake on one of the train seats, as now there was plenty of room. We didn't have time to get any breakfast in the Kansas City depot, so we ate sandwiches for our morning meal. It didn't make any difference to me, though, because no matter what my mother put on the table, it always looked plenty appetizing. My dad went into the dining car and had our thermos filled with coffee. He brought back three small bottles of chocolate milk for Lois, Pat, and me. At home we mixed Hersheys' Chocolate with Dinah's milk for a special treat. We had never had chocolate milk from a creamery before, so this was very special.

My dad looked at us while we were munching on our sandwiches and chicken and riding across the countryside. He remarked, "Now, isn't this living?" We all smiled and nodded our heads.

As I ate my sandwich and drank my chocolate milk, I saw a man riding a horse by a little creek. It was some scene.

Then I noticed that there was absolutely no snow on the ground. I couldn't believe my eyes! No snow in December! No snow in the wintertime! I said to my dad, "Look, Dad, they don't have any snow here!"

He said, "Billy, we're down South now; it's a heck of a lot warmer here than that tundra, Littlefork!"

We rode and rode, crossing the countryside. We saw a lot of poor people; in fact, they looked to be even poorer than us. Most of the people were Blacks. Lots and lots of Blacks lived in little shacks alongside the railroad tracks. Many of the people were sitting in rocking chairs on their porches just rocking away as we went by. Many of the little Black kids waved to us. We had no Black families in Bemidji or Littlefork.

All of a sudden out in the middle of nowhere the train stopped. All of the Black people on the train picked up their suitcases, shopping bags and the rest of their belongings. I asked my dad where all of those people were going. He whispered, "Shut up!" I didn't ask any more questions because I knew he meant business.

When all the Black people left our car, my dad explained, "This is the Mason-Dixon Line. From now on Black people can't ride with us. They have separate cars, toilets, and sometimes even stores to shop in. They have all gone to another car where they will ride from now on."

I didn't say a thing because I didn't want to make my dad angry again. I wasn't sure how he felt about all of this, but I knew for certain that the sisters of St. Philips in Bemidji would agree with me that this was very cruel and wrong.

That evening we ate our sandwiches and chicken again. Our lunch was still holding up quite well, except that my mother's bread was starting to get hard and dry. I asked my dad if we could have some more chocolate milk. He said, "No," but that tomorrow at noon he was going to take us on a real treat and that we were going to have dinner in the diner. I remembered the words in a song, "Dinner in the diner, nothing could be finer," and began singing it softly as we plowed through the dark of the night.

Every so often the train would slow down and when it did, I would have to know why. I would slip out of my little nest and rush to the window whenever I detected a change in the train's speed. I would cup my hands against the pane in order to get a good view of the southern towns or the snowless countryside. When we came to a complete stop, I could get a good look at some of the railroad workers or people gathering to get on or off our train. I always waved to the people and most always received a wave back. One depot agent even winked at me. Too often, our train would stop, go backward, then forward again which meant that we were leaving the main line and going onto a sidetrack to let the more important and faster trains go by. I would then have to scoot across the aisle and sit by my sisters in order to get a good view of the passengers in the faster train. These people appeared much richer; my dad called them big shots. I hoped that someday I'd be a big shot and take my entire family on a trip across the United States. We would travel on the fast trains only.

All of the sounds and smells associated with riding the train were beautiful. "All aboard!" or "Boooaard!" the conductor would shout prior to our leaving each station. Muffled bits and pieces of men's conversations were constantly picked up by me. The rattle of the cream cans or the sounds of the cream can wagons being pulled across the brick depot platforms were very pleasant sounds to my ears.

When we hit the outskirts of Dallas, Texas, the conductor entered our car bellowing, "Dallllas--Commmminn Up on Dalllass--Next stop for passengers getttin' off at Dalllasss." As he walked through our car, he rocked and sashayed back and forth in his beautiful blue uniform trimmed with bright gold buttons. The title, "Conductor", was printed in gold letters above the bill of his hat. I wanted to be a conductor in the worst way someday, but my dad always said, "No railroad for you, Billy!"

It was such a wonderful feeling as I looked out the window as we approached the various towns. Prior to entering the automobile crossings, our engineer would blast his whistle, "WAHH OHH WAHHH, WAHH OHHH WAHHH"; and then just as we entered the crossing, the signals would flash, "RED-RED, RED-RED, RED-RED", keeping perfect time with the bell that said, "DING-DING, DING-DING, DING-DING". At the very same time, the black and white wooden arms would automatically go down so that no cars could possibly run into us.

Throughout the night the whistles, bells and man talk would fade in and out of my mind, "WAHH OHH WAHH, WAHH, OHH WAHH, DING, DING, DING, DING, DING, AMARILLO, AMMMARRILLOO, NEXT STOP, AMMARRILLOO, FOLKS GETTING OFF AT AMMMARRILLLLOO, CLICKETY-CLACK, CLICKETY-CLACK, CLICKETY-CLACK".

While I lay in my little bed, I thought about my father's elk's tooth, and what the southern families who lived alongside the tracks were like. I wondered if their Christmases were as happy as ours. Did their children have a grandma who knitted them some mittens, a grandma who bought them pop and played whist with them as an equal partner? "DALLAS, DALLASSS, CLICKETY-CLACK, CLICKETY-CLACK, DING, DING, DING, BOOOOARD, ALL ABOOOAARD!" Would Uncle Charley be at the San Antonio Depot to meet us? Would he recognize us? Of course he would. We would be the only ones dressed in caps, coats and overshoes and our shopping bags said "St. Paul" on them. Yes, he'd recognize us alright!

All night long we had oodles of room. I put two of our suitcases between the walkway of my seats and then managed to curl up in the seat with my legs resting on the suitcases. I made a terrific bed for myself. My mother put her white rabbit fur coat, which I cherished, over me. I didn't have a care in the world as we bounced along towards San Antonio.

I could see both of my parents sitting in their seats across the aisle. My dad was stretched out in his beautiful blue suit. He still had his vest on, and his gold railroad watch was in one of his small pockets. Dangling on his watch chain was his elk's tooth that Mom bought him for Christmas. It cost $5.95 and it was very, very beautiful. Above the tooth was a clock and it read eleven o'clock. I asked my dad a couple of times what that meant; and he said, "When you get to be an Elk, you'll know; it's a secret!" I remember learning from the sisters at St. Philips that one couldn't belong to a secret organization. When I asked my dad if it was a secret like Uncle Oral's Masons, he said, "Shut up and don't talk about it anymore." As I dropped off to sleep, I wondered about that clock on my dad's elk's tooth saying eleven o'clock.

The next morning I woke up with a terribly stiff neck. We were beginning to look travel weary. My mom's hair was all out of place. My dad looked like he needed a shave, and Lois' and Pat's eyes were full of sleep. Their hair needed combing. I was ashamed of all of them for a little bit; but then, when I looked around the car, I noticed that no one else looked much better.

I was really getting very hungry, and I was glad to hear Pat and Lois whine about wanting to go to the diner. I could tell that it was getting time for us to go as my dad was getting somewhat uneasy.

My dad decided to have a rehearsal on how we were to act and what we were going to say while we were in the diner. He laid down the rules and we listened carefully. "Now, when we get in there," he said, "I'll look the menu over and tell you what we're going to order. And eat everything on your plate. Remember, do what I do and don't gawk at the Black waiters!"

As he talked, he began to get angry; and the longer he schooled us, the angrier he became. Finally, we all marched through a number of other coaches and eventually entered the dining car.

When we arrived, a Black waiter greeted us with a very friendly smile. He took us to our table and asked my parents if they wanted to start things off with a cocktail or a cup of coffee. I was happy that there were very few people in the dining car as I wasn't sure we would do all the right things.

The tables were all set; each table had at least three or four layers of pure white tablecloths. There were all kinds of dishes on the tables including the silverware, which was beautiful. I could tell we were all in trouble when I spotted three forks and two spoons for each person. I wished my dad had schooled us on the silverware.

The waiter gave us our menus; even though I was a good reader, I found most of the items were strange to me. My dad asked the man if he was still serving breakfast. He replied, "Noh, suh. It's lunch time now!" I looked at my sisters, and I knew that they, too, wanted to start laughing when we heard the Black man talk. We did everything to maintain our serious faces as we had never heard southern people talk.

My dad said we would all have a cheese sandwich and a bowl of vegetable soup. I couldn't believe it! A cheese sandwich, I hated them! But I could see that it was the cheapest thing on the menu. No one said a word until my dad broke the silence by saying, "Well now, this is really living, isn't it?" "Yes," we all agreed and nodded our heads up and down. Personally, I was scared to death that I might spill or slurp my soup. I knew one thing for sure, we didn't belong in there. I wished the lunch we packed in Littlefork would have lasted longer.

Finally, after we drank a lot of water, the waiter brought our cheese sandwiches and our vegetable soup. Our sandwich came on a big, beautiful plate. There was a little piece of lettuce with a half of a peach by our sandwich. The sandwich was cut into four pieces. A nice blue toothpick was pushed into each quarter piece of the sandwich. I was careful to watch my dad as he had said to watch him if we didn't know what to do. It was then that I noticed that he had already tucked the white cloth napkin into the front of his shirt right by his Adam's apple. My mother, Pat, and Lois had done the same. I quickly put my napkin in front of me, too. It looked funny to see us with our napkins covering our fronts. It was the first time ever I remember having used a cloth napkin. Even when Bill Shawton came to eat, we didn't have cloth napkins. The waiter made many trips to our table. Our soup came with a silver cover placed on top of the soup bowl. All of those dishes rested on a much larger plate. I had never seen so many plates and bowls and silverware for just a cheese sandwich and a bowl of vegetable soup.

During most of the time while we were eating, we went over some rough tracks. It was tough to keep from spilling every spoonful. My dad commented that his track was never that rough.

When we were almost finished, the waiter came back and said, "I'll bet everyone is ready for a little dessert. We have some fine pie in the kitchen. How about you, my little man, would y'all like a nice piece of apple pie?"

I nodded that I would. I completely forgot about waiting for my dad's cue; but when my dad said he didn't think he cared for any because he was too full and my mother and sisters said they were all filled up, too, I knew then that I had forgotten my father's briefing.

When my pie came, the waiter said, "Here's that apple pie for the little man." Then he looked at my parents and sisters and said, "Are y'all sure I can't get you something sweet now?"

My dad said, "We would sure like to, but we don't know where we'd put it. We're just filled to the brim. Maybe later this afternoon."

I knew everyone else wanted a piece, but it was the money. I also knew that we were not coming back later this afternoon as my dad had said.

When the waiter brought the bill, my dad opened his wallet and placed a ten-dollar bill on the little black tray. Our cheese sandwiches cost 85 cents each, the soup was 60 cents a bowl, the coffee, 15 cents a cup, and my pie was 50 cents.

The total bill was $8.05. My dad left 25 cents on the tray for the waiter's tip.

When we got back to our coach, no one said a word. I just looked out of the window. My dad said from across the aisle in an angry singsong fashion, "Well, would the little man like another piece of pie?"

My answer was, "No."

He asked, "Didn't we go over all of that? Didn't I tell you to keep your eye on me and that I'd do the talking?"

"Yes," I replied.

He continued, "Then why didn't you do what we had agreed to do?"

My mother interjected, "Henry, people are listening."

My dad said, "Margaret, that's highway robbery! That little lunch cost us $8.05! Why, that's terrible! And he didn't need that pie any more than the rest of us. Why didn't he look at me?"

Just then the conductor came up to my dad's seat and said, "I hear you work on the N.P. up in Minnesota."

My dad smiled and replied, "That's right. I'm the section foreman in Littlefork, Minnesota."

The conductor said, "I have a distant cousin living in Littlefork; I wonder if you know her."

They started talking about the conductor's relative and right after that began a lot of railroad talk. Was I glad that the conductor came along!

"Wasn't that something when we finally got to Texas," Pat commented. "Remember when we went to the drive-in movie and Dad sat back in Uncle Charley's car smoking a cigarette? The volume box was attached to the car window, and Dad said, `Boy, this is living! I wonder what the poor people in Littlefork are doing now?' And remember when we went down to the marketplace and bought a trunk load of pink grapefruit and sweet potatoes to ship back home? We ate grapefruit and sweet potatoes until they came out of our ears," Pat added.

"Yes, Texas was something else with the Alamo, Spanish Gardens, and the zoo. We really did it all," I agreed. "Uncle Charley couldn't believe I remembered so much; did he ever laugh about our dinner in the diner."

Moments later Pat continued, "And weren't Father Riley's words something else?" Lois and I agreed. "He was beautiful. He got a little carried away, but Dad would have been as proud as a peacock."

My mother came from the kitchen with several sheets of paper in her hands. "Father Riley gave me Dad's eulogy," she said. "Bill, do you want to read it."

I took the yellow pages and began reading. "I would like to take this occasion, as a personal friend, as pastor of St. Colomban, and as a citizen of Littlefork and the area, to extend my sincerest and heartfelt sympathy to the grieved family, to his aged mother, to his devoted wife, to his children and their families, to his brothers and their families, and to his friends and acquaintances. Accept our condolences; accept our prayers. All of us here feel, along with you, that we have suffered a deep personal loss in the passing of Henry Kirtland. We know that only the white bandages of time and God's supporting help will cure the wounds of grief.

"It is not difficult to be mindful of our dead in the days of great grief immediately following upon their departure from us ..."

I stopped reading and said, "You know, Mom, while Father Riley was reading the eulogy in church, I wondered who was going to become his special friend. Who will be the one who will slip into the confessional and pose as a traveler going through Littlefork? Remember when Dad pulled his coat over his shoulders and said, 'Bless me Father for I have sinned. And Father, I just robbed the Littlefork Bank of $10,000. Father, please forgive me!' And Father Riley quickly replied, 'Henry Kirtland, the Littlefork Bank has never had $10,000. For your penance you are not to smoke a cigarette for two weeks!' And how the two of them laughed!

"And Grandma Kirtland was there. How in the world can a mother stand to bury her son? It must have been plenty tough on her. Once in a while Dad used to talk a little unkindly about her; but when one of us said anything critical of her, we sure heard about it. Dad always talked about how she would read detective magazines all day; and when she would hear Grandpa's speeder coming by the section house, she would run, set the table, put a kettle on the cook stove, and then put a cold wash cloth on her forehead. When Grandpa came into the house, she would say to him, `Oh, Bert, I have had such a terrible day with my headache and all; but I've got supper on the stove, and it'll be just a few minutes. Maybe some bologna sandwiches and some hot vegetable soup would go pretty good on your hard-working day. Bert, what do you think, sugar?'"

"Bill, keep on reading the eulogy!" Pat demanded. "We have to get to bed."

I continued reading, "It is in the rays of these golden hopes that we lay the mortal remains of Henry Kirtland to rest, knowing that dying to the world he lives in Christ.

"His life was Christ-centered when he lived. His end was Christ-centered when he died. He encountered Christ first in baptism, becoming an heir of heaven, a brother to Christ. In confirmation he met Christ, the soldier, and from Christ drew the strength to live his Christian beliefs. In the confessional he encountered Christ the merciful, humbly asking forgiveness for human failures. At the communion rail he tasted of the bread that came down from Heaven, the `Bread of Angels,' finding in the body and blood of Christ the spiritual food to feed his soul. In the sacrament of matrimony he met Christ of Cana of Galilee who blessed the marriage contract and became the third party to his life-long association with his wife, Margaret. In his final illness he met Christ again, this time the `Divine Physician' who came to him in the last anointing to give him the comfort and the courage to walk that last long, terrifying mile from life to eternity."

My mother said, "I hope the Good Lord is really merciful to Henry. He always meant well. I hope the Lord will excuse his swearing and his stories. And what did Father Riley say about his tolerance?"

We all grinned. "Did he say he was tolerant of another's religion, politics, or point of view?" Lois chuckled.

"Hopefully the Lord will forgive him for telling his favorite of all stories," I added. "You know the one about the Irishman who sold the Swede two large round rocks shaped like eggs for 50 cents each. The Irishman said that if the Swede would sit on those two eggs for one hour a day for 27 days, he would hatch a small pony. So the Swede gave the Irishman a dollar for the rocks, and he began to faithfully sit on them.

"On the 28th day the Swede looked for the ponies but there were none to be found. On the 29th day, he checked his nest again; but there was still nothing, no ponies; and on the 30th day when he still had no horses, he decided he had been tricked by the Irishman, so he took the two rocks out behind the barn and threw them into a brush pile.

"When the rocks hit the brush pile, two jack rabbits jumped out and started running for the woods. The Swede ran after them hollering in his pronounced Swedish brogue, `Whoa dare, whoa dare you, knuckleheads; don'tcha know your fodder?'"

We all laughed. We laughed heartily! "My gosh, I haven't heard that story in ages. Dad did love to tell that story," Pat sighed.

"Here, let me finish the eulogy," I said.

"By design, I have spoken of Henry Kirtland's loyalty. Loyalty to cause and people was a brilliant feat in the sterling character of this man. He was intensely loyal to his Church, to his religious convictions. He would defend his own beliefs to the death; yet, he never debased himself by criticizing another man's religion, be he Lutheran or Baptist, Presbyterian or Anglican. In politics, he was a fierce promoter of his own candidates; yet, he never stooped to ridicule the opposition. In heated discussions, peppered with his Irish wit and humor, he accepted others' opinions. In his employment he demanded his personal rights; yet, his loyalty forced him to give his best to his employers at all times. In his friendships, and who can count them, a closeness, a sympathy and intimacy, a loyalty that made him one with the suffering, made him one with the jubilant. In his family, he displayed a loyalty that showed itself in tenderness, in concern, in sacrifices, in love. All who have known Henry Kirtland are a better man or woman for that association. Henry Kirtland will live in the hearts of man for a long time to come.

"Thus love and respect for him will forge the final strong link in the ties that bind us to him. Love does not perish at death. If we have loved him in life, that love can no more cease to exist at death than God can cease to exist. May the deeds of love continuously unite us, the living and the dead. Our prayers, our sacrifices, our sufferings, and our grief can help to speed the souls of our departed friends into the dazzling light of God's presence. On their part those in eternity intercede for us with Christ, Who is the Resurrection and Life before the Throne of God. In this band of love we are still one with Henry Kirtland.

"May he hear from the lips of his divine Master, `Well done, good and faithful servant. Enter into the joys of the Lord. I am the Resurrection and Life; he who believes in me, even if he shall die, shall live, and whoever believes in me shall never, really die.'"

As I put the eulogy on the end table, I could hear the freight train coming up the tracks from down by the depot. We all began to feel the rumbling and shaking of our section house. Tears ran down my sisters' and mother's cheeks. I walked over to the three of them and extended my arms around them. The four of us sobbed as we hugged each other for strength.

"Toot! Toot!" whistled the train as it went by.